Poisoned Lies

5 Tales of Damnation

Autumn Blair

Published by AJM Publishing.
Visit us on the web for more great books:
http://ajmpublishing.net

First Printing, 2014
Printed in the United States of America

ISBN-10: 1942283059

ISBN-13: 978-1-942283-05-8

Table of Contents

Shady Manor

Jess, like everyone else in Blissfield, knew the legend of Shady Manor. You couldn't live in a town with less than five thousand people and *not* know about it. She stood outside with her ticket in hand, waiting with her boy-friend, Scottie, to take their run through the now haunted house. It was their first year participating be-cause Jess wasn't exactly fond of having the life scared out of her. Dark, spooky places terrified her and it did-n't get any darker or any spookier than Shady Manor. Rumor had it that a girl who'd lived in the house with her family had murdered everyone. Part of the rumor was that she'd played the game *Clue* and wanted to act it out.

"I can't wait!" Jess' best friend, Stevie said, gripping her shoulders and giving them an excited squeeze.

"I couldn't tell." She rolled her eyes and sighed.

"Oh, now don't be a buzz kill. We've been waiting for this since last Halloween."

"Seriously? There's so much more to look forward to than Shady Manor. Fifteen minutes and it's over."

"Fifteen of the scariest damn minutes of your whole life." Zach, Stevie's current fling chimed in. "Hey, let's go, it's our turn."

Jess turned around to see the large black curtain looming in front of them. Taking hold of Scottie's hand, she took a deep breath.

"It'll be alright Jess. Like you said, fifteen minutes and it's all over," Scottie whispered, smiling and planting a kiss on her cheek.

Together, they stepped into Hell on Earth. The smell came first, pouring over you in a thick wave so that breathing became difficult. The stench of death was so putrid that Jess could hear Zach and Stevie trying not to lose their lunch in front of them. Holding her hand over her nose, Jess slowly crept along the eerily lit hallways. Flashing lowlights in red, green, blue and silver gave each turn a compliment to the gore that threatened to scare the life out of you.

"Ah!" Stevie screamed. Jess inhaled, gripping her best friends hand tighter. Around the first corner Jess watched as a casket came flying towards them. It hit the wood platform and toppled over, pouring thick mud and disgusting looking body parts everywhere.

"Holy shit," Jess whispered. Unlike Stevie, who screamed when she was scared, Jess held it in, panic and fear making her that much quieter. Barely able to see Scottie in front of her as he pulled her along, Jess followed bravely. Again Stevie screamed, with Zach hollering close to the same time.

The second turn was a showcase of zombie's gorging themselves on human intestines, their mouth and hands covered in blood. Jess looked ahead for Scottie but, when she looked back, a zombie was pressed against the glass; growling at her, reaching for her.

"You're next," blew a whisper that sent a chill down Jess' spine. Turning, she only saw thick fog and the flickering of lights. Still following close behind Scottie, Jess felt something grab her hair. Shivering, she turned and, again, saw nothing.

She hadn't heard Stevie or Zach in quite a while and wondered if they'd finished the maze already. Scottie didn't seem to hear her either as he continued to drag

7

her along with him. The third turn brought Jess and Scottie to a large cemetery scene; the smell of dirt clinging to the air. Walking through it, Jess would have sworn she felt things crawling with her, grasping at her feet and ankles. At the last grave they passed Jess stumbled when a hand reached out to grab her leg.

"Fuck!" Jess yelled, tightening the grip on her boyfriend's hand. Violently kicking at the fingers wrapped around her ankle, Jess managed to get free from the mechanism. Continuing along, Jess and Scottie finally came to a fork in the maze. The left was lighted; a path to the exit she supposed, for those that weren't enjoying having the shit scared out of them.

"You wanna go this way?" Scottie asked, his eyes hopeful and full of excitement.

Shrugging her shoulders, Jess decided that it couldn't be that bad. Before moving through the first door, participants were asked to pick a weapon. A scythe, a sword, a dagger, the replica of a pistol, a javelin, cross bow, etc. They seemed to have a weapon for just about every occasion. Jess tried to refuse, but gave in when a knife was thrust into her hand. Again, they moved on, Scottie in front, barely visible in the crappy lighting.

"Do it," came another whisper, floating through the air. Jess pulled the knife up, closer to her midsection.

"You know you want to." This time the voice was in front of her, emanating from a creepy old woman. She had a hideous face, decrepit from years of torture. Her skin scarred and infected. When she smiled with a gut wrenching cackle worthy of a 1980's remake, her grotesque teeth were revealed. Jess turned away, as if seeing was enough to believe. Real or not, the person playing the witch was in sore need of a breath mint.

Jess walked along, still unable to see much. Finally lowering the knife, she came upon a long hallway decorated much like the long hallway in the movie The Shining. They'd even scrawled REDRUM along the back wall, with strobe lighting making it hard to concentrate. Jess was starting to grow weary of this house and its odd infrastructure. No house she knew of could be built like this.

"A hundred cuts, bitch," came a harsh, nasty voice. Jess heard the distinct sound of a blade pulling from a scabbard. Seconds later, she felt a slice on her arm. Raising it to the light, she saw a long slice across her skin; her blood slowly seeping from it.

"Son of a bitch." Frustrated, Jess wrapped a handkerchief from her outfit around the wound. Suddenly, she felt Scottie's hand tighten on hers, urging her to hurry. "I'm coming, hold on."

Scrambling, Jess picked up the pace, trying to keep up with her boyfriend. No matter how fast she moved, Jess still struggled to keep pace; his hand still tight on hers she called to him. "Scottie, wait. Slow down!"

Scottie's hand went lax in hers, her body finally able to slow down a bit. "Sorry," came Scottie's voice, a tremble running through it.

"It's alright. Have you seen Zach or Stevie up there anywhere? I haven't heard them in a while, so I'm thinking they got out early."

"Yeah, I don't know. We'll find them on the outside, don't worry."

"Fine. Can we get out of here now?"

"Almost, let's go this way." Three more spooky turns and Scottie and Jess finally found a doorway with EXIT scrawled across it in big, bold, red paint. Scottie smiled at her in a way that made her heart skip a beat. Leaning in, he kissed her on the cheek again. Shivering, Jess stepped through the doorway.

"Freeze!" Jess heard the command; her eyes still adjusting to the intense brightness outside. Hadn't they gone in when it was night time? How the hell was it the middle of the day? Jess took another step, still blinded by the light. "I said freeze! I'll shoot if you don't hold still."

"Drop the knife lady!" rang another loud, male voice. "Drop it now or I'll shoot!"

Jess dropped the fake knife in her hand, hearing the distinct clatter it made against the wood, the clatter that a real knife would make.

"Get on your knees, and then lower down to the porch on your belly. Put your hands on your head with your fingers interlaced."

Jess did as she was asked, still trying to figure out if this was part of the experience or not. It seemed like well over fifteen minutes had passed. Jess felt the footfalls of people on the porch with her, felt someone take her hands off her head. It was really when they put the first handcuffs on her that she realized something was horribly wrong. Looking over, she saw Scottie just standing there. "Scottie?"

"I'm here Jess. No worries, this is great isn't it?" Scottie said, squatting down so she could see his face. "You're going to love the ending."

Assuming that he was right and that this must be part of the experience, Jess smiled. She was read her Miranda rights and put in the back of a police car. She was immediately relieved when she looked and Scottie was sitting next to her. She noticed that he wasn't in handcuffs, but blew it off as another part of the fun. "I'm not sure I like this part so much Scottie. It seems a little too real."

"Just wait," Scottie encouraged her. "You're in for a real treat."

***

The drive to the station was silent. The only sound came from the police scanner and posts the dispatch made to other units. Jess was extracted from the police car and actually booked into the jail, fingerprints and all. She was quickly escorted, along with a smiling Scottie to an interrogation room, where she was handcuffed again, this time with the cuffs in front of her. She looked around the room, locking her feet around the legs of the chair in a way she'd done since she could remember.

Trying to relax she looked at Scottie who was leaning against the wall smiling.

"You like this don't you, you sick bastard?" Jess said, starting to feel anxious. "You like seeing the shit scared out of me. You know I hate dark spaces and yet you had to pick Shady Manor."

"Oh come on Jess." Scottie chuckled. He moved to sit on the table facing her. "You can't tell me that you didn't like it, even just the slightest."

"The best part of that whole thing was getting out." Jess replied, her lip starting to tremble. "Now I'm here and I can't tell what's real anymore. This seems a little intense for something that's supposed to be a Halloween joke."

"No worries, Jess," Scottie assured her again. When the door opened and two detectives walked in, Jess noticed that Scottie went to stand over by the wall again.

"Miss Standish, this is detective Matthews. I'm detective Anderson," a tall, relatively handsome man said as he sat down across from Jess. Automatically, she pulled her cuffed hands into her lap, frightened. "We need you to tell us what happened between the hours of ten o'clock last night and two o'clock this afternoon. Let's start with where you were."

Jess took a moment and thought about ten last night first. "Scottie picked me up about nine. We met Zach and Stevie who were going to Shady Manor with us. We got there about nine thirty, had to wait in line forever and then took our turn in the maze. I couldn't hear Zach and Stevie much after about the first half of the maze so Scottie and I figured they must have taken the early exit." Jess paused, noticing the way the detectives looked at each other.

"Go on Miss Standish."

"Well Scottie, I could tell, really wanted to finish the maze so I said okay. When we got to the second section of the maze they had all of these fake weapons laid out and made us each choose one. I tried not to but someone put a knife in my hand. We went through the second part which, admittedly, was a little spookier than the crazy scary first half. Then we finally reached the exit and came out. Have you asked Scottie about his version of the events? I could barely see him in the dim lighting. The only reason we stayed together is because he wouldn't let go of my hand."

"Is he holding your hand now Miss Standish?" the older detective asked, his brown eyes curious.

"Of course not, he's standing over there," Jess replied, pointing to Scottie. Both detectives looked up and stared blankly at the wall. "Scottie, why don't you tell them what happened."

"Can't, part of the rules Jess."

"Oh for Pete's sake, just tell them. I want to go home now and they don't look like they're playing along anymore. Please," Jess pleaded, starting to tremble.

"Now Jess, you know I can't do that. It'd ruin all the fun you're going to have. I promise it's going to be mind-blowing when it all ends," Scottie promised, squatting near her and taking her hands. He kissed them and Jess shivered.

"Why are you so cold? I feel cold whenever you touch me now."

"That's pretty normal for me. Don't you remember?" Closing her eyes Jess saw him now, inside the manor as he moved through the maze. The images that flashed through her mind were horrific, terrible and gruesome. Pages out of a horror story that slipped through Jess' mind like a reel.

Opening her eyes, she turned her horrified gaze on the two detectives. "Please tell me this is all a Halloween prank."

"Afraid not sweetheart," the younger detective answered, pulling large pictures from a folder he carried. Laying them out on the table, he told Jess the story behind each one. "Shady Manor, as you call it, has been closed for years. It was a swanky bed and breakfast when it first opened, some pet project of a rich and famous couple. Then it became a psychiatric ward for people with moderate to severe mental disorders. On its last leg, the building was turned into a sort of haunted house. That shut down as well, nearly three years ago. Miss Standish, do you have any idea what happened in that house last night?"

"I told you, my friends and I went into the maze, but when we went in it was dark and when Scottie and I came out, it was the middle of the day today. It was only supposed to be fifteen minutes. How did it jump entire hours?"

"You said your friends went in with you, but you never actually saw them, did you? When you came out, that is."

"No. I heard someone shout *freeze* and Scottie said it must all be part of the show."

"Can you describe Scottie for me?"

"I don't have to describe him, he's standing right there." Jess pointed again.

"Indulge me," the detective asked, looking down at the pictures. Jess looked now, too, seeing faces among the gore of the maze now. At first it was all a blur, the faces, the maze, the gore, all of it muddled together. Then she saw Stevie, her face still, lifeless. Her throat slashed, gruesomely from side to side. Zach came next. His face was eerily still as well, his eyes having been gouged out. When Jess found Scottie's face in the pictures, the tears came like a flood and what little she'd had in her stomach followed.

"What the hell is happening?" Jess choked out in a whisper. Scottie came over then, kneeling next to her as she bent over from the waste. "Please tell me what's happening."

"You're not dreaming Jess, since that's what you're thinking. No, you're not dreaming. This is as real as real gets, honey," Scottie told her, but when Jess looked at him this time it was the gruesome face from the picture

17

she saw. Shaking uncontrollably, Jess shut her eyes tight. She turned then, opening her eyes to the two detectives.

"You don't see him do you? You don't see Scottie standing there?" Jess asked, already seeing the answer in their eyes.

"No," The detective replied grimly. "Our records indicate that four people went into the Manor maze, only you came out Miss Standish. When we processed the scene, we found three victims inside, all with some sort of knife wound. It looks like Stevie, as you call her, was the first; Zach came quickly behind her. Scottie, as you refer to him, was the last one to die."

"How..." Jess asked, her words barely audible. "How did Scottie die?"

"He was sliced, ma'am, as if someone wanted him to suffer. So far the coroner has counted at least a hundred cuts over the surface of Scott Duncan's body.

It flashed through her mind again. "A hundred cuts, bitch." Jess pushed the pictures away. Looking over at Scottie, whose face was back to its normal self, was watching her, his blue eyes intense, sorrowful. He came closer to her now, squatting next to her again.

"I think you snapped, honey," Scottie said, continuing. "You found out that Stevie and I were sleeping together behind your back and went a little crazy. You forgave us, or so we thought. You seemed fine, as if nothing had happened. When you suggested we check out Shady Manor for Halloween it all seemed legit. We were all looking forward to getting the crap scared out of us. We just didn't know that you had other things going on in your mind. When Stevie screamed that last time, it was because you cut her throat, Zach's eyes came next. By the time I found them they were already gone."

"What did I do to you?" Jess asked through her sobs. He smiled now, resting his brow to hers. "You were so angry with me and who could blame you really? In the dark, even with my eyes well adjusted, I could barely see my hand in front of my face. I felt the first slice along my cheek, the second on my arm, the third along my neck. You were fast, efficient and a crazy. Every time I tried to catch you, you were already moving around me, cutting me as you went. Some of them were superficial, but the ones that counted cut deep. One slice across my wrist cut a vein; I was losing blood faster than I could stop it from pouring everywhere. When I dropped to my knees, you laughed. You said, "A hundred cuts bitch, for the hundred you placed on my heart." It's the last thing I remember.

"But…" The memories came flashing back like a wave.

"Miss Standish?" The detective said, placing a gentle hand on her shoulder. Jess looked at the man with haunted eyes, hers having dulled considerably.

"I'll do whatever I need to do," Jess offered, seemingly resigned to her fate. She spent the next hour explaining what Scottie had told her. Between bouts of hysterical laughter and uncontrollable sobbing, Jess explained how she'd found Stevie and Scottie together. She'd shut down the emotions then, telling her friends that she forgave them, that she understood how passion could flare between two people. She explained the now clear and horrifying events that took place inside Shady Manor, how she'd convinced her friends and boyfriend to go along with her to "Spook Fest," by promising them the scare of their lives. She explained in minute detail how she'd gone after Stevie first, because they'd been fast friends and the hurt had felt like having her heart cut out. Zach was collateral damage, Jess had said. She couldn't let him live, witnesses weren't allowed. Scottie she saved for last. She'd loved him and he'd ripped her heart out by sleeping with her best friend. She'd wanted him to know pain, how what he and Stevie had done, had hurt her.

"I didn't know how I was going to do it at first," Jess continued to explain. "I knew I wanted him to suffer. I wanted him to hurt as much as he'd hurt me. When I cut him the first time I knew then that it would be slow and painful. That was good and right."

"So how did you start thinking about it being a dream or maze when we found you?"

"I don't know. I could still see Scottie clear as day when my eyes adjusted to the light. Even when I came here he was still with me, still promising that it was all part of the plan, that I'd love the ending." Jess laughed now, with no humor filling the sound. "He was right about one thing. It's certainly mind blowing."

Jess signed her statement and dated it. She was charged with three counts of first degree murder with special circumstances.

***

She still saw Scottie, his eyes dull, no longer bright and excited. Stevie and Zach thankfully didn't haunt her the way Scottie did. Perhaps it was because she'd finished them quickly. She'd tortured Scottie, so maybe it was her penance that he stayed with her.

She'd see him often, most of the time when she was alone, but rarely did she talk to him. He never spoke first, but would answer a question if she posed it. "Are you part of my imagination?" Jess asked him one night when she was first given a jail cell.

"Not entirely," Scottie replied. "Part of me, the part you see, is imagination. I look like this because it's how you choose to remember me. My body is worm food now."

Jess moved on, tears filling her eyes. "Why did you sleep with Stevie?"

"I made a stupid choice," Scottie admitted, continuing. "When I first thought about it, I told myself that I could never do that to you. Then I realized that she'd thought about it, too. She made it pretty obvious. One night, she called and I went over to see her. That was the first time it happened. After that, it seemed easy, as if we'd never get caught. As irrational as that seemed, I realized it wouldn't last forever and when you found us together I was so relieved. I didn't have to hide anymore. Both Stevie and I were surprised by how laid back you were. Neither of us suspected anything when we went to Shady Manor. You'd made it seem so crazy fun that we all decided it was worth checking out."

"When did you know?"

"What, that you had planned to kill us?" Scottie asked. Shrugging he added, "I didn't know. I was as lost and as alone as Stevie and Zach. When I realized what was happening you'd already started cutting me. When you slit my wrist I knew then that Stevie and Zach were probably dead, as well. I knew I wouldn't be leaving that house alive."

"I'm going away for life you know?" Jess said, having resigned herself to the idea that she'd never again see the light of day for freedom. Her sentencing came quickly after her guilty plea. Standing before the judge with her feet and wrists shackled, Jess awaited her fate with her free attorney standing at her side. She knew Scottie was there too, although she saw him less and less now. She sort of worried about the day when she never saw him again. She didn't know whether that would mean she was no longer crazy, or had jumped off the cliff into complete insanity.

"In all my years on the bench I've never dealt with a case quite as gruesome as this. You, Miss Jessica Standish, will get the most extreme extent of the law that I am able to give you. Because of the heinous nature of the crimes you committed, I have no choice but to sentence you to life without the possibility of parole.

You will be remanded to the Pestell County Jail until proper transference can be arranged."

Jess was once again led away and rode stoically back to the jail. Scottie sat beside her. "So, what now?" Jess asked, irritated that he wouldn't just leave her to her thoughts.

"Now we wait. It won't always be this bad, you know. I can't exactly speak for Stevie and Zach, but I've already forgiven you. I knew what I'd done drove you to snap. If anyone's at fault its Stevie and I for betraying you."

"It's all in the past now. The only thing I have to live for is to try and make some sort of restitution to your families."

"Nah. You know my parents are conceited and self-centered assholes. Stevie's parents barely notice she's around and Zach hasn't lived at home in more than two years."

"That doesn't mean they won't care that you all died."

"Well of course not, but seriously, restitution isn't necessary. Eventually, like all loss, our families will move on with their lives and, while they may never truly heal, they won't always hurt the way they do right now."

Arriving at the jail, Jess noticed that Scottie wasn't anywhere to be found. Once she was in her jail cell though, he appeared again. "Whose hand was I holding in the maze?"

"What?" Scottie asked, his dull eyes brightening.

"I asked whose hand I was holding. If I supposedly killed you, Stevie and Zach, then whose hand was it that I was holding walking through that shithole?"

"It was mine." Scottie assured her. Except it wasn't really attached to my body anymore. When you cut my wrist it went to the bone. The next swing came quickly taking it off completely. By then I was pretty far gone, I may have screamed but if I did it wouldn't have sounded very loud."

"That doesn't make any sense." Jess said, her head hurting from all the questions. "How would I not notice I was carrying around a hand that I hacked off my boyfriend?"

"Shock, I guess. Maybe by then you'd started to realize that not everything was as it seemed."

"What's my favorite color, Scottie?" Jess asked, almost desperate.

"Blue, obviously. I gave you that blue cardigan for your birthday last year."

"When's my birthday?"

"Seriously? June 12, 1992."

"What's my favorite position?"

"For what?" Scottie asked, appalled. "For sex? God, Jess. You like to be on top, I guess."

"Wrong!" Jess squealed. "You're not my Scottie. He would know that I'm traditional and always prefer missionary."

Ghost Scottie rolled his eyes. "So that's your basis then, for saying I'm not your Scottie."

"I don't have a fucking clue what's happening, but you're not my Scottie. So get the hell away from me!" In an instant, the apparition who'd called himself Scottie was gone.

***

Alone in her cell now, Jess could hear sounds through the silence. Screams and loud yelling were faintly reaching her ears. They grew exponentially louder the closer she leaned towards them. Looking out through her cell bars all she could see was her own reflection in the glass across from her. But, looking closer, she realized that it wasn't her reflection she saw, but someone else altogether. Raising her arms up and down, twisting her head side to side, sticking her tongue out, the woman in the reflection did all the same things, but it sure the hell wasn't Jessica Standish staring back at her.

After an hour of rattling her cell a guard finally came by. "What the hell's happening to me?"

"You're in prison honey. Happens to all of us sooner or later. You're an expedited case though."

"What does that mean?"

"It means that you are an exception to the rule. See, around here, we have early arrivals, people who off themselves for one reason or another. We have those who arrive on time because someone else offed them or they died in some way. Then we have expedited cases. People who are sent here as a punishment for a crime they committed above, such as your case."

"You mean I'm dead?"

The guard grinned with a devilishly snare. "Absolutely, doll."

Eternal Torment

Katherine pushed the button on the coffee maker for the second time. The first had been nearly an hour earlier when she'd made her now favorite cup of mocha espresso. With that fresh dose of caffeine buzzing through her system she'd made and packed three lunches straightened everything in her husband's briefcase and was just calling the girls to wake up when James walked into the kitchen. A quick kiss on the cheek with a "Good morning," thrown in and it was off to business as usual.

"Sherry!" Katherine called up the stairs as she started to climb. Waking her girls in the morning was like being a battering ram. The two oldest especially could sleep through a tornado, unless they were doing something particularly fun, then it was 'up and at `em.' "Come on sweetheart, it's Monday again and you my dear, have school." Shaking her oldest daughter gently, pulling dirty blonde locks of hair from around her daughter's neck. Katherine moved on to Mindy, moving her daughter's white-blonde hair away from her face, she planted a kiss on the kindergartener's cheek. "Let's go tiny mite, it's time to open those pretty blue eyes."

"Hmm." came the throaty sound of waking from her second daughter. Knowing her work here was done, Katherine moved to her own room where her youngest girl was just waking up. "Hi Mama." came a tiny voice when Ella came bounding off her toddler bed. At just two years old, Ella was the most rambunctious and headstrong of Katherine and James' three girls. Unlike her two older sisters, she sported copper colored red hair that curled in the cutest ways. She was big on her "finger curls" and let everyone know it. She had blue eyes like her sisters, the famous gene passed down from their father. Sherry was tall and lean, lanky like Katherine had been as an eight year old. Mindy was shorter and thicker, with curves that Katherine knew would be trouble in another ten years.

Poking her head into her older girls' room, Katherine was satisfied that they were up and getting dressed. With an hour to go before they left she knew that they'd all be ready and piled into the van on time this morning. That hour went by like a whirlwind and before she knew it her three munchkins were scrambling toward the van, their lunches in hand. Stopping them at the door, Katherine loved each girl in turn, holding her oldest two longer than she knew they preferred. Sherry was on the cusp of womanhood, but Katherine held on to the little girl she still was today for an extra moment.

"All right Mom," Sherry lamented, stretching up to kiss her mother's cheek one last time before she booked it to grab her favorite seat in the van before her little sister took it. Snagging an arm, Katherine scooped Mindy up into her arms for a bear hug the little girl was famous for.

"Be good today," Katherine admonished, rubbing her daughter's nose to give the Eskimo kiss that the two used as a gift of affection. Putting her daughter down, Katherine watched her bound happily toward the van. Always the peacemaker, Mindy wasn't the least perturbed that Sherry had gotten their equally favorite seat first. She simply picked another and sat down to buckle her seat belt.

"Pick me up, Mommy," little Ella asked, her tiny arms stretched in front of her. Katherine did so, giving her tiny terror an extra big squeeze.

"You have fun at Aunt Tarran's today and be good."

"Okay Mommy," the little girl promised. Katherine put her down instead of carrying her to the van. Like her sisters before her she liked to run as well. Katherine was about to follow her out when James caught her hand.

"I'll buckle her in," he said, pulling Katherine close. His blue eyes, just beginning to line with age, smiled down at her. Answering that smile Katherine stretched on her toes to bring her lips to his. The kiss wasn't long, or deeply passionate, but in that moment Katherine felt all the need and hunger that swam through them. "I love you Katherine."

Reaching up to touch his face, Katherine returned the endearment and watched as her husband walked to the van, snuggling their youngest daughter before playfully plopping her down in her seat. He was so good at that, taking that tiny moment to make her giggle while the other two clamored just as much for his attention. He tickled their middle daughter, making her giggles ring through the air. Then he kissed her brow, admonished her to sit back in her seat. Tipping Sherry's chin up until their matching blue eyes met, James flicked a finger down her nose, being instantly rewarded with a smile. A kiss to her brow as well and the van door slid shut. Turning, James waved to Katherine who returned the gesture, before he climbed behind the wheel. He started the engine, putting the van in reverse to back out of their driveway.

Katherine turned back to face her home which would take at least an hour to clean up just from breakfast. With her coffee cup in hand, she took a step toward the kitchen when a loud smashing sound had her turning back toward her front door. Looking out the window Katherine saw the horrific scene as if someone had dunked everything in water. Blurred and smudged Katherine could barely make out the van that had her family packed lovingly inside. Its side was caved in deeply by the SUV that had plowed into its metal framing. Shaking, Katherine opened the door and ran, reaching the van in mere seconds. Opening the other sliding door, Katherine succumbed to the shock that engulfed her. Her middle daughter, who'd loved life to the fullest lay unmoving, across the backseat, her seat belt stretched taught. Sherry, her body battered by the metal that had crumpled during the crash had been thrown out of her seat, her seat belt torn and hanging limp. Katherine, tears pouring from her eyes, rocked back and forth as her hand reached to feel for a pulse. When Katherine couldn't feel that tiny beat of life, she lost the breakfast she'd made that morning. Working frantically now, as if she could turn back the clock, Katherine checked tiny Ella, who was also not moving. Gashes across her daughter's head and face bled profusely and as Katherine looked, those tiny blue eyes didn't register a thing. More sobs racked Katherine, as she stretched behind the little girl's seat to touch her middle daughter's face.

"Mindy, please God, don't take them all from me!" Katherine sobbed. Her fingers barely reaching her little girls' neck.

"Ma'am?" a gentle voice said. Katherine didn't register the hand on her arm, still trying to reach Mindy. "Ma'am, it's okay. Let me check her." Katherine turned then, her grief ravaged eyes so full of tears that she couldn't make out a single feature on the man's face. "Why don't you let my friend Stacey here bring you over there? We'll take care of your girls for you."

"They're going to be late for school now," Katherine said, her mind simply overwhelmed by her loss. "My husband, they were all on time this morning, too. I should've known. We're always running behind." Katherine talked to Stacey as three tiny body bags were wheeled over and gently placed in the coroner's van. James, who'd also been pronounced dead, took a little longer as Katherine had needed to see him.

"Please don't leave me," she'd cried, holding him as her body shook with soul wrenching sobs. "I can't do this without you." She'd finally let them take him and her girls to the morgue. Her in-laws had come within the hour and sat with her, equally as grief stricken. Katherine had moved through the house like a ghost, calling James' name and asking him if they should have chicken or steak for dinner. She called all three girls as well, her mind simply unable to deal with the grief of losing her entire family. The next week was much the same. Even with her in-laws patiently trying to deal with her shock, Katherine refused to see life as it was now. She couldn't bring herself to accept anything less than her family being alive and well.

"Sherry!" she called on Friday. "It's time to get up for school. Today's the last day of the week. You'll be able to spend the night at Aunt Tarran's and Uncle Rick's house." She pushed the button on the coffee pot again, brewing the large pot that would serve her and James this morning. Turning Katherine saw her mother-in-law making breakfast.

"Thanks Mom," Katherine chirped. "The girls will love a hot breakfast. Although, Mindy will surely give you a fit over the eggs. I'll put some on to boil for her." "Katherine," Sarah said, her voice soft, gentle. "Katherine, there's no need to put any eggs on for Mindy, sweetheart." Going to her daughter-in-law, Sarah pulled the woman close and just held on. "Mindy won't need them this morning, honey. And Sherry, James and Ella are doing just fine, too."

"What do you mean?" Katherine asked, trying to step back. "Of course they'll need breakfast."

"Not today, dear," Sarah said, her own voice straining with the tears that filled her eyes. "Today, they need you to love them. To love them enough to let them go and come back to us."

"What do you mean let them go?" Katherine asked, the ever present fear flooding her system.

"Oh, Katherine," Sarah said. "It feels like forever that you've been stuck here in this house, in your grief. As a mother and grandmother I know the grief is overwhelming, saturating. I know that most days it steals my breath before I can even think to breath. I know that your heart isn't simply broken, it's shattered into a million tiny pieces. I also know that James would be heartbroken to see you this way. To see you stuck in your grief like this. I know that Sherry, Mindy and Ella would miss their mama." Sarah had to take a minute to swallow the tears. "We all miss them terribly, Katherine. And, for us, we miss you as well. You are still here and we need you."

Katherine saw the grief in her mother-in-laws eyes, felt the heart clenching pain in her own soul. "I don't know how to live without them," Katherine whispered, tears flowing over onto her cheeks. "I miss them so damn much." Sarah gathered her close as Katherine simply crumpled to the floor. The keening sobs pierced through the denial, through the soul stealing hate that Katherine wanted desperately to hold on to.

The funerals finally took place the next week. Katherine was nearly inconsolable as her family's bodies were laid to rest. She spent four hours at their graves, watching as the dirt was poured over the caskets. She touched their headstones, talking to each of them as if they were standing in front of her. She cried, reaching for the healing that still seemed so far out of her grasp. Her mother-in-law left with Tarran and Rick, but John, her father-in-law, stayed behind, patiently waiting for her. Finally Katherine rose and turned around. John opened his arms and gathered Katherine close, both of them shedding more tears. Katherine allowed John to tuck her into the passenger seat. The ride home was silent, she and John both lost in their own thoughts.

Sarah and John hosted family and friends that had stopped by to give their condolences. They graciously, and gratefully packed away the casseroles and ready-to-heat dishes that were kindly left behind. They stayed another week with Katherine, patiently watching her new routine. She no longer called their names. The door to the girls' room had been closed and Ella's bed had been left alone as well. Katherine hadn't been able to bear moving a single item. As the week went on though, she seemed to get better with each day, moving past the mind numbing pain.

Bolting awake at 6am, as if her body was adjusted to a new clock, Katherine made a thermos of coffee and drove to the graveyard. She sat with James, Sherry, Mindy and Ella as the sun started to streak across the sky. "It's so beautiful here. Do you remember the time you took me to the beach, the night you asked me to marry you?" Katherine whispered. "That's right girls. Your daddy was a romantic, although I don't think he wanted anyone to know it." Katherine smiled then, re-membering the night she'd become the future Mrs. Hines. "Then there was the day we found out that you were coming Sherry. You were such a blessing to us. You were the first to make me a mommy." More tears came now, the grief still ever present. "You were so bright, but so afraid. You'd cry if a stranger said any-thing to you and I remember the first time we tried to get you to play in finger paint. You wouldn't touch it until your daddy got down with you and showed you that it was okay. Then your little sister came along and you became a big sister. You were mesmerized by Mindy, until she started walking and talking. Then reali-ty set in and you weren't so pleased to have her around. There are so many memories of you. Swinging in the big red baby swing before you could handle the big girl swings. Fighting over your toys and play fighting when it wasn't the real thing. I miss you so much." Katherine cried quietly for a while before she talked to Ella. "You were quite the surprise little girl. We tried for ten months before you finally came along. I was sure you were a little boy, you made mommy so miserable in those first few months. So different from your older sisters. Then you came squalling into the world with all that red hair and an attitude to match. I miss your tiny voice and those precious little hands. You three girls were the light in my life. I miss your daddy too."

"She's healing now," came an oddly cold voice into Katherine's ears. Turning she looked around the graveyard. Nothing. She turned her attention back to James' grave. Caressing it she said, "I miss you. I miss all the love we shared, the intimacy I couldn't share with anyone else. I miss my best friend so much. I still don't know how to do this without you, without our girls. Your mom and dad have been wonderful, not to mention Tarran and Rick and the kids. They hold me up when it's all just too heavy. I still haven't gone through anything. I don't open the girls' bedroom. I don't sleep in our bed anymore. I spend most nights on the couch pull out in the living room. I keep the fire going all the time because I always feel cold. I drink coffee all day so I won't sleep. There's a hole in my soul that I can't fill James. It hurts so much sometimes. Then I remember you, or the girl and it doesn't hurt quite so bad. The pain is bearable now, although I don't think it'll ever truly leave. I can't wait to be with you again. I'm not suicidal so please don't worry. I just know that when my time comes, I'll face it with a big smile because I'll be coming home to you and our girls. Please take care of them. They still need their daddy, especially until I can be with you again. I don't feel right yet, so I'll keep coming back to visit until I do. I love you all."

***

"She's back to the good, sir," a young servant said, keeping his head down, low. He never looked the leader in the eyes, never thought to challenge the man's dominant role.

"I want to see her," the Leader said. "I need to know where that good keeps coming from. Humans are fickle creatures, right? They bend when the wind blows and cower when the challenge is insurmountable. Everything good was stripped from her and yet she keeps finding good in it."

"Yes sir," the servant agreed. "If you'll follow me sir..."

"I'll make my own way. Prepare the ninth circle. If the seventh isn't doing its job, I'll pass her along. We'll keep going deeper until I've stripped the very soul from her body."

The young servant slipped away silently, doing as he was told. The Leader neared the young woman's cell. Much like a jail cell, the walls were made of stone, solid with barely any room for light. The cell door however allowed the Leader to see his captives fully. More than just their bodies he wanted to see inside their flesh to the heart of their being. It was their souls he wanted most of all.

The woman he was observing now was a constant pain in his ass. No matter how many times he turned her back, how many times he made her relive her worst nightmare, she always seemed to find the good in it. How the hell was he supposed to gain her soul if she always found the good in what he showed her, the pain and agony, the loss and grief? She'd been reliving it for years now and still she found good.

Reaching through the bars of her cell, he brought her roughly forward, slamming her body against the burning cell door. The agonizing scream was like music to his ears. She might find the good in the midst of her nightmare, but this reality was a bitch to wake up to.

"You will love the ninth circle, if you think this one's good," the Leader said, his dark, lifeless eyes boring into her. Those once bright, hazel eyes were dulled by the pain of her physical being. But it was inside those eyes, straight to the soul, that the leader was looking. Eyes are the windows to the soul, after all. Her soul, no matter what he put her through, seemed to hold on like a cold when summer had finally arrived. It was ruthless in its search for goodness. He'd found over the years, dealing with thousands, millions of humans, that it was the will that was hardest to break. You could crush their emotions; devastate their minds with disease and grief, circumstance. It was that will, though, that he found the hardest to break.

He'd been successful, no doubt about it. He had thousands of cowering and fearful humans who'd finally

40

been broken down by the constant torment he loved to put them through, but for all those he'd broken he had a hundred times more that he was still working on. He'd even had to add an eleventh circle of torment and punishment to his layer just for those that were dogged in their determination. He released the woman he'd held, watched as she dropped to the floor and turned to see the humans around her. Some of them were screaming in the midst of their nightmares. Others had finally woken to their new reality and were still in the first stages of shock. Still, others sat crying, sobbing. Hoping beyond hope that it wasn't real. He enjoyed those. They were like a treat when he'd fasted too long. Each time one of them started to grasp that reality, he knew he was close to securing another soul. When they finally let go and gave up the ghost, it was an emotional high like none other.

"You'll never have me you sick son of a bitch!" the woman he'd tortured spat at him. He saw defiance in her eyes now, the cold, calculating hate he'd come to expect since Cain killed his brother Abel. Now, *that* had been entertaining. Humans were so full of contradicting emotions. It was always a joy to watch them fall from their highs. The landing was always a smash.

Smiling, he looked the woman in the eye. "Actually, I never had a mother. I was once an angel, but that job got boring. I much prefer my form of employment now. It's so damn gratifying. I can still make music, you know. Beautifully haunting tunes that speak of all the evil in the world. And the real estate isn't bad, either.

Earth might just be a rock in the galaxy to some, but to me it's a gorgeous piece of property that I rule. You puny humans might think its "Mother Earth" or whatever, but it's mine and always will be.

When the servant came back, the Leader sent her on to the ninth circle without a second thought. He'd make his rounds; send others down farther if they needed a fresh perspective of their living nightmare. As for her, she'd learn the harsh reality of her fate. The ninth circle would strip even the hope of good away from her nightmare. She'd relive the deaths of her family. She'd know the grief and agony, the overwhelming loss, the defeated sense of sorrow. Maybe then she'd give up her soul and finally be done trying to dig her way out of the hole she was in.

⁎⁎⁎

Katherine felt the sweltering heat of her new cell. The other place had been hot, this was skin blistering. Slumber seemed like a better alternative and so Katherine gave herself up to sleep. She woke, rested, in her house. The alarm was blaring and six-thirty flashed across the clock. Pulling herself out of bed, Katherine wandered downstairs, pushing the button on her one-cup maker to start her espresso. The day ran as usual and the crash came again as well. She once again ran, like all the other times, to rescue three little girls that were already gone. She sobbed over her husband's body as the coroner and medical personnel worked to secure the scene and the bodies of her family. The grief came now, swamping

42

her, saturating every fiber of her being. The hate came too. She watched the EMT who was working on the other driver, desperately trying to save his life. Furious, she ran, knocking the EMT off his game. "You don't get to save him today! He killed my entire family. He doesn't get to live today!" Katherine spat, rage coating every word.

The EMT, sympathy swelling in his eyes, shook his head once, but quietly stepped around her to continue his work. Drained, Katherine slumped to the ground, watching the man fight for his life. "It's not fair, you bastard! You took my life from me. What do I live for now?" Katherine found less good this time. Gone were the loving in-laws who'd loved her and patiently drawn her out of her grief. Gone were the friends and extended family to hold her up. Without that she sank into the depression that wanted to swallow her. Consumed, Katherine attended the funeral for her family quietly alone. She raged against their headstones, angry and full of bitterness. Her body crumpled under the grief and she eventually woke once again in the ninth circle. Her damnation much easier to grasp now. Still she went back under, reliving it again and again. The good was so much harder to find, but her soul struggled for even that glimmer until it found it.

Within a week's time Katherine found herself in the eleventh circle, where the heat penetrated her body to the bone, making her feel as if she was burning from the inside out. Sleep came quickly as a source of escape. But the nightmare was so real, so fresh, that it wasn't escape at all. It was simply trading one hell for another. The nightmare came, just as it had the countless times before. This time though she watched as her children's bodies were battered and tossed through the van. She saw the moment each of them expired as if she'd had a front row seat. She knew the last thought on her husband's mind, that he wanted her, even as he turned the wheel and the SUV plowed into the side of the van. The piece of glass that had hit him in the temple had cut his thoughts short and stolen his life, *their* life. Still, she knew he loved her, had loved her till the very end. That was good and hopeful.

"You retched bitch!" the Leader called, yanking her from her nightmare. "Why won't you just give up?"

"As long as there is a shred of hope for me to cling to, you'll never have me."

"Maybe the nightmare should change then. Maybe it shouldn't be that your family died. Maybe it'll be that your husband was screwing around on you."

"You can paint whatever picture you'd like, and I'll find hope in that. I know my family is gone. There's no coming back from that. But you, you are a bastard and I'll die before I ever give myself to someone like you."

He laughed now, the full bellied cackle of someone who knew the ending to a joke that hadn't been told yet. "You don't know, do you?" More laughter now. He nearly doubled over from it. "Come here. Open those blind eyes." Passing a hand over her face, the leader showed her the immenseness of the eleventh circle. "You're already dead, Katherine. I keep running you through the nightmare of your life on Earth in hopes that you'll eventually give that sad soul to me, but this is your reality! You'll never escape from this, no matter what you find in the hopes of your worst fears. The best part is that no matter what that reliving looks like, you'll always wake up here. There is no happy reunion with your family, there is no seeing your daughters or husband again. That hope you thought you had back there was as useless as tits on a frog. Take that into your next round, because when you wake up you'll be right back here with me and your factual reality."

And again, Katherine slept her nightmare.

Siren Fog

Derek for one, couldn't wait for his parents to finally walk out the door. They were like toddlers, always having to grab one more thing before they could make their break for whatever boring, work related bullshit conference they were headed to now.

It wasn't that he didn't understand. He knew that they were doing the responsible thing, but he couldn't help wondering, because that's what twelve year old boys do, whether they did it for themselves, to be away from him for a while, or whether it was truly about the money they'd be making. He could admit that he liked them being able to afford a nice house, two sweet cars and anything he asked his parents for, but sometimes he wasn't sure whether they really loved him, or whether they were just tolerating him until he turned eighteen.

He smiled lying on his bed up in his room. He'd heard their car start and actually pull out of the driveway. He'd loved them goodbye three trips back to the house ago.

47

They'd made no effort to do it all again and neither had he, once was enough thanks. Pulling his already filled pack from under his bed he took out his brand new cell phone and dialed Kyle, Eric and Ben. All three guys were up for a weekend in the woods. Derek had packed enough shit for the four of them to stay in a coma like state of sugared bliss pretty much the whole time. He had soda, marshmallows, chocolate, graham crackers, six full size candy bars, gum, pop-tarts, bread and peanut butter. He'd even remembered to pack a knife and a roll of paper towels. He'd also packed extra clothes, his sleeping bag and pillow, and a whole pack of Marlboro Red cigarettes he'd lifted from his dad's stash. The man was clueless and would never even notice.

Strolling up to the end of his street, Derek saw Ben and Eric headed his way. He turned to the right and saw Kyle as well. Once everyone arrived, the four of them set off to the west. They'd have to cover some ground in order to get Kyle's five man tent set up before nightfall. Derek for one was thankful that Ben and Eric, twins by all accounts, had remembered the soda. Just outside of town, Derek lit a cigarette, take a chocking puff when the tip turned red. He coughed for what seemed like forever, but took another puff anyways. He passed it to Kyle who did virtually the same thing. Ben and Eric politely declined, laughing raucously at their two friends.

The sun was just beginning to set as the boys reached the edge of the woods. Stepping into the clearing they got their first look at the Benton Cemetery and Crematorium. Fog covered most of the ground in a thick layer of puffy white, so that the boys' systems were already full of adrenaline and excited nervousness. They worked quickly with Ben and Eric searching for firewood while Kyle and Derek set the tent up. They tossed everyone's sleeping bags inside with the food and soda. Derek lit another cigarette, as they sat on a log they'd pulled over from another part of the edge of the woods, offering it to Kyle who accepted. They didn't cough as much this time and Derek considered that good progress. It wasn't long before Ben and Eric returned, their arms full of sticks and twigs for the fire. All four boys plundered the nearby woods for large rocks to build the section for their fire. They scrounged for nearly half an hour before finding enough rocks to make it work.

"We'll have to dig into the ground a bit," Kyle said, putting the first rock in place. Using his hands Kyle dug down a few inches around, creating a space that would keep the fire contained. The other three boys place the rest of the rocks in place and Kyle set to work building the teepee style chute that would allow the smoke and heat to rise and keep the fire going well until it caught. He took Derek's lighter and using a few wrappers from their candy bars, set the small twigs on fire. The flames caught well enough and soon the boys were roasting hotdogs and marshmallows over their little fire.

"This is the best man," Derek said wholeheartedly. He polished off his hotdog and automatically reached for a marshmallow, blowing it out when the flame caught it. He smashed it between the chocolate square and a graham cracker smiling before he took the first bite of his s'more.

"We're gonna remember this Halloween for the rest of our lives!" Kyle agreed, giving a whoop as he bit into his own delicious goodie. Ben and Eric quickly followed and the boys spent the first hour of nightfall gorging themselves on junk food and warm soda.

Lying back the happy four-some were quiet for a minute while they watched the stars come out to shine in the night. The moon was appropriately full and huge as Halloween officially got under way. Sitting up Derek asked his friends, "Anyone know any good ghost stories? Cuz I've got one if no one else does."

"Please tell me it's not the one about the hot nurse you *saw* during your last hospital stay," Kyle begged dryly, waiting with a wry smile for Derek to pop him for bringing it up again.

"No, but if you want I can rearrange your face for you. I did see her and she was smoking hot, not that you'd know what that looks like," Derek defended.

"You think I've never seen a porno?" Kyle retorted, his own temper growing right alongside Derek's.

"Oh for Christ's sake shut the hell up," Ben and Eric chimed in unison. Derek and Kyle looked at them. If was so weird the way they did that, always finishing the others sentence and shit. "Who gives a shit if you did or didn't see something. A smoking hot girl is different for all of us."

Sitting back again Derek and Kyle both cooled off some. "Now, Sarah Hinsley, for instance is way hot, even if Kyle thinks she's a dog."

Kyle chuckled, covering his mouth in a display of youth they all still had. "She's so ugly dude. I wouldn't set her up with my actual dog, let alone a friend."

"Say what you will man, she's hot and she's got boobs. Every other girl in our class is still waiting for puberty to hit. Give her another year and I'll be able to motorboat those babies."

"Like she'll pay your limp dick the time of day," Kyle shot back, earning him a not-so-light punch in the arm.

"Shhh," Derek ushered, sitting up and looking toward the fog. "Did any of you hear that?"

"Hear what?" Ben asked, just a quiver of fearful anxiousness touching his voice.

Derek sat up straighter, straining to see through the smoking white haze. It came again a little louder, calling his name. "Derek Decker," Derek scrambled back, away from the wispy fog.

"You heard that, right?" Derek asked; his soft brown eyes huge as he looked at his friends.

"Dude, there's nothing out there except white fog and long dead ghosts," Kyle assured, laughing and slapping his buddy on the shoulder.

"Still, maybe we should call it a night," Derek suggested, crawling like a crab backwards towards the tent. He narrowly missed burning his hand on the hot coals of the banked fire. He didn't wait for his friends to join him. One look at the thickening fog was enough for him to wait inside the only shelter they had.

The other three boys looked at Derek and back at the fog, wondering why the kid was freaking out on them. Kyle, deciding it was harmless stood up and walked into the fog until he could barely see the tent of glowing coals of their fire. "Look, Derek, I can barely see where our fire is and nothing's happening to me."

Derek watched through the screen of the tent as fingers appeared in the fog. He watched them slither their way around Kyle's slender body. Nervous sweat ran down his temples, making his hands clammy. Kyle's name ran screaming through his head as the hands moved over his body, wrapping slowly around his neck. The only scream they heard though, was that of Kyle as his body was yanked ruthlessly into the abyss of the fogged over cemetery grounds.

"Holy Shit!" Derek squeaked, as Ben and Eric hurriedly joined him in the tent. "Guys, we can't go out there."

"What the hell was that?" Eric sputtered, looking worriedly at Ben and Derek. The three friends waited, barely breathing for any sign that Kyle was coming back. An hour passed before any of them really moved.

"How long before sunrise?" Ben asked, scared and exhausted now from worrying and watching the fog.

"Nearly seven hours." Eric said, looking at his watch, an exact copy of the one Ben was wearing, except his was black with orange ribbing, where Ben's was orange with black ribbing.

"Damn it, I can't last that long," Ben lamented, burrowing himself down in his sleeping bag, curling into the fetal position.

"Go to sleep you pussy. We'll stand watch until Kyle gets back. Then that asshole can take a turn." Derek said, angry and not completely sure why.

Ben tried hard to sleep but every time Derek or Eric made a sound he'd open his eyes to see what was going on. Giving up, he moved to get a better vantage point of the cemetery and everything else his brother and friend were looking at. He was the first to see Kyle moving slowly, oddly through the fog.

"Hey, you three idiots," Kyle replied slowly, "I hope you saved some good shit for me."

"Kyle?" Derek asked, still not believing it was his friend. "Holy crap, dude. I thought you were a goner for sure. That fog looked crazy and I heard you scream. What the hell happened?"

"I wanted to scare the shit out of you is what happened. Never seen you move so damn fast before." Kyle laughed, but Derek heard the difference in it. Back up, he moved Eric and Ben behind him, lit a cigarette, as if he didn't have a care in the world. Moving to the opening of the tent, Derek stuck his hand out, "Want a hit?"

His friend looked at the cigarette with imagined interest. "Nah, those things'll kill ya."

"Ha. I knew you weren't really Kyle, although you look enough like him." Derek smiled, pulling the cigarette back into the tent and pulling a drag from it. "Kyle would have taken the offer."

"So who are you?" Eric asked, his voice shaking.

"I'm the ghost of Christmas present, bitches." Kyle smiled, his eyes glowing a sickly shade of red. "I'd tell you what happened to my body, but it'd take too much time, and since I only have tonight, I might as well make the most of it."

What had once been Kyle, reached out and simply tore the tent open. He had Eric by the scruff of his neck within seconds and was lifting him off his feet. "Hello there, Eric. I thought you'd like to see what it's like, this living death."

"No, seriously dude, I'm good just as I am," Eric choked out, squirming helplessly to get free.

"Seriously, you think this existence that we had is better than what I can give you?" Kyle asked with a sickly smile. "Always knew you were an idiot. Let me show you." One quick jerk of Kyle's hand and Eric's body slid to the ground. Derek went white as a sheet and Ben lost his dinner, vomiting where his brother would have slept that night.

"Ben, get the fuck out of here." Derek whispered, too afraid himself to move an inch. "Now!" Ben looked over at Kyle and nearly pissed himself. He scrambled out of the tent, tripping over the log and falling face first. Kyle's larger than life hand reached him quickly.

"Uh, uh Ben," Kyle sneered. "In a minute your brother here is going to wake up and tell you that I was right all along. None of us are getting out of here undead to-night. The fog, it calls to me like a siren. Listen closely and it'll call to you too."

"I just want to go home man," Ben pleaded, tearing running down his cheeks.

"Well at least Eric didn't cry or beg," Kyle told them. Chuckling, he brought Ben close to whisper in his ear. "You'll love the ecstasy of escape, bro. Not to mention that anything you can imagine can be yours. Remember Sarah Hinsley, whom you're so fond of? You'll be able to have her when I release you from this pathetic excuse of a body."

"Please, please just let me go. I won't tell anyone what happened here, I just wanna go home." Ben felt Kyle's grip soften, felt his feet touch the ground again. Looking over he watched as Eric rose from his body that was still lying on the cool ground. "Look what I caught, Eric. Your little brother isn't so sure he wants to join us. Should I let him go or show him what it's like?"

Eric looked at his brother, his twin by less than three minutes. "Ah let the little douche bag go. He'll run to mama. Not that she'll believe a word he says." Kyle did as Eric suggested and Ben ran screaming from their campsite back to the railroad tracks that led into town. He had no idea that getting back to town before he died of hypothermia would be a very close call indeed. Eric, still newly dead, sort of hoped his twin would make it. Before he could regret his death too much, Kyle turned toward the tent and the lone occupant inside. "Derek, you little skank, get out here."

Derek poked his head over the canvas. He watched as the ghosts of his two friends came closer.

"It's true what he said, you know?" Eric smiled. "I can be anywhere I want, whenever I want. Right now, I'm talking to you, but another part of me is sitting, well floating really, right outside Sarah Hinsley's bedroom and man is she fine. She undressing and sweet god if she doesn't have the sexiest titties I've ever seen."

"Idiot," Derek thought, shaking his head. "She has the only titties you've ever seen, you douche."

"True enough, but what about your dream girl, don't you want to see her again? I'm sure if she's as real as you say she'll be ready and waiting buddy." Eric smiled, knowing he had his friend on the hook.

Derek could admit that the idea was a curious one. Looking now at his two friends though he knew there was no coming back if he stepped over the line. "What happened to you?"

Kyle smiled. He knew Derek well enough to know that his friend wouldn't be quite so easily convinced or persuaded. When I stepped out into the fog, I could hear it calling my name, just like you said. I ignored it though, so bent on scaring you guys. I felt it slithering over me and I saw the fear in your eyes, I think, because I was already gone in my physical body anyways. The moment the fog grabbed me I was lost. It's a crazy ride for sure dude. But I can tell you that if what you saw was a ghost, there's only one way to find her again."

Derek wrestled inside the tent. At twelve years old he knew his parents no longer saw him. They left money on the table if he let them know he needed it, they signed papers he left for them without reading them. He was basically on his own, making the best decisions he could at the time. Why not see what it was like on the other side? He'd still be alive in a way. Sure he wouldn't have a body, but what did that matter? He'd just live eternally as a twelve year old kid who could do whatever he wanted, and if the nurse he'd seen did exist on the other side, he knew she wouldn't have a problem with that, if her actions in the hospital had meant anything. Who would really miss him, because he certainly could-n't say he'd miss his life.

"Alright, dickheads," Derek gave in, stepping from the tent. "But, I want the fog to take me, too. If I'm meant to die tonight, it might as well be from some supernatu-ral bullshit."

Kyle and Eric smiled, knowing what Derek was in for. The instant terror and flash of pain before death took over. They watched as Derek stepped into the thick wispy white. He stood still waiting as the fog swam around him. He watched Kyle and Eric's eyes change. Kyle's turned to a glowing red and Eric's to a glistening white. As the fog snatched him from his body, Kyle and Eric's head were jerked upward, the light from their eyes shooting to the sky. Derek's first non-living breath was pungent, acrid sulfur in his nose and mouth. Looking down, he saw his lifeless body sitting upright close to Kyle's. Eric's he knew, was still slumped by their ruined tent.

Joining his friends Derek quickly learned the ropes of the being dead. He had an obligation now, to haunt anyone who was dumb enough to come around near All Hallows Eve. He thought fleetingly of Ben, but the thought flew away when Derek felt a presence behind him. "Hello again." Turning, Derek saw the young woman who'd visited him in the hospital.

"You're here." Derek smiled, turning to gloat to his friends. "Told you she was hot."

"Well shit, Eric," Kyle retorted with a purely male grin. "Looks like Derek lucked out after all. Well done my friend."

Derek smiled a toothy grin. "I tried to tell them that I wasn't hallucinating that day."

"Oh no. I was sad that you didn't come to me then, but I can see by the looks of you that I was fortunate you decided to wait. Let's blow this place for a few hours. We'll have to be back before long, but we've got a little while yet." Derek smiled again, a young man on the verge of adulthood who couldn't wait to see what his little naughty nurse wanted to show him. Kyle and Eric watched as the girl and Derek faded from view.

"Should we?" Eric asked.

Kyle laughed, smacking Eric on the back. "Nah. Let's let Derek have his fun, hopefully it'll be us some day." Kyle played around the edges of the woods, scaring animals and the wandering stranger or two that walked in the woods on the spookiest night of the year. **Didn't people know that restless spirits were the most active tonight?**

Eric spent another ten minutes watching young Sarah Hinesly change into her pajamas before he headed for his own home. He found his parents easily enough, sitting at the kitchen table chatting over coffee. Ben, as he presumed he'd be, was in his room with all the lights on, practically shivering under his covers. His first transition through the solid construction of his parent's home was quite something. It was odd to feel himself coming apart and then back together again.

Himself once again, or as close as he was going to get to it anyways, Eric sat on his brother's bed. "Hey pussy." Eric laughed, as Ben pulled the covers up further. "Oh for Heaven's sake. Just take the blanket off and look at me. I'm not going to do anything to you, you little douche."

"Screw you, Eric," Ben scoffed. "How the hell am I supposed to explain to our parents that you're dead, not to mention Kyle and I have no idea what's left of Derek."

"Easy. Just tell them that all you knew about was us going camping. You felt bad and didn't want to come. They'll find all our bodies out there. Kyle's and Derek's are close together, as they were both taken by the fog. Mine is exactly where you saw it fall. They'll never know that you were out there."

"Will to, I puked in the tent when Kyle snapped your neck." Ben shivered, "Holy hell Eric. Do you have any idea what this is doing to me?"

"No, but hey, at least you're still alive. Someday you'll know what it's like to get married, have sex, and have babies and a life. All I know is what it's like to think about those things. I'll never actually have them, experiences like that."

"Get the hell out, Eric. I hate you and I want you and your buddies to leave me the hell alone."

"You got it, idiot," Eric replied, obliging his little brother for the last time.

***

Ben Ringold pulled up to the empty space and parked. Pulling on his pack, he set out into the woods, walking a path that he'd have known in his sleep. He pulled a cigarette from his pack and lit it up. He had no idea what was pulling him to do this idiotic thing. He hadn't been back here since that night and truthfully he wasn't sure he was looking forward to it. All Hallows Eve was a night when weird, creepy shit tended to happen. Still, he couldn't help but hope he'd at least catch a glimpse of his childhood friends.

He set his tent up, built a fire that he lit as the sun started to set. He ate dinner and waited as the first stars streaked across the sky, marking the start of the scariest night of the year. The dark overwhelmed everything once the sun set completely and Ben watched as the fog lay in a thick layer over the cemetery, just as it had the night his friends and brother had died. They'd found their bodies just as Eric had told him they would. It was ruled a homicide but Ben was the only one who really knew what happened. He said what Eric had told him to and no one had ever been able to prove otherwise. Ten years later, Ben still knew exactly how he'd felt that night.

At twenty-two he'd done most of the things Eric had told him he would. He knew what it was to feel so crazy in love you'd do just about any dumb ass thing a girl asked you to just to prove it to her. He knew the ecstasy of sexual bliss and the terrifying wait when a girl you'd been with told you she thought she was pregnant. Thankfully no baby had come his way as yet. He wanted to wait a while on that one. He was going to ask that girl he'd fallen in love with to marry him. He had the ring all ready and waiting. This last weekend would clear up the rest of the fog in his head. He'd move on to the rest of his life with a clear conscience, his friends safely tucked into his past.

"Well holy hell boys. It looks like Ben decided to finally grace us with his presence." Derek chuckled. "Honestly, I didn't think you had it in you buddy. It's been ten long years and we hadn't seen hide nor hair of you since that night."

"We were beginning to think we'd all lost our minds," Kyle chimed in, crossing his arms over his broad chest.

"H-how..." Ben stammered, confused. "How are you guys grown up? You all died that night when we were twelve."

Kyle laughed, slapping his leg in a way that made Ben reminisce about that night. "Died? We're as alive as we've ever been buddy. It wasn't us that died that night, Ben, it was you."

Looking up, Ben saw their faces, each wearing the same humored expression. "What?" Ben asked. "I didn't die. Kyle was going to kill me, like he had you Eric, but you told him to let me go. You said I wouldn't tell anyone and wasn't worth the waste of your time."

"Ugh yeah, but that wasn't about letting you go, it was about leaving you behind. On the way through the woods, you slipped on the wet grass and landed on a log that had a jagged edge stick out of it. You died the instant you hit that stick. We were all so scared that if we didn't finish the weekend out that it'd happen to us."

"Y'all are crazy. How do you explain Elizabeth? I met her at a convention. I'm asking her to marry me next weekend."

"She's a figment of your imagination buddy," Kyle explained. "Look at yourself, do you look older than you were?"

"Of course I am. I'm almost twenty three, which is how old you douche bags would be if you hadn't been so dumb."

"Look, either you believe us, or you don't. It doesn't matter in the least because the fog is out for vengeance tonight," Eric said, looking at his little brother. Twins or not, he was older and in family that's what mattered. "We came by to see if you'd be here. We never figured you'd show up thinking the same thing. So how do we figure this out so we can all get back to our lives?"

"Headstones, idiot. If we're dead, the headstones would say so. If Ben's the dead one we'll know that, too." Derek said logically. The four once-upon-a-time friends scanned the headstones, searching the cemetery for any of their names.

"You weren't buried here, Eric," Ben told him, remorse showing on his face.

"Then where was I buried, since I'm not the dead one?" Ben pointed and like a flashpoint all four friends were at another, smaller cemetery. The ground there was equally foggy as All Hallows Eve moved along. They looked over the stones and Kyle, Eric and Derek started to laugh.

"You idiot. Read the name on this stone." Ben did so and felt the hot, sharp pain of shock slide through his system. Looking up though he realized he recognized other names; his parents, sister, Eric, Kyle and Derek.

"We're all here," Ben confirmed, rubbing his chest. "How the hell are we like this if we all died back then?"

***

Like a projector all four friends were transported back to the night of All Hallows Eve when they were average twelve year old boys who thought they'd gone camping. Watching from above the boys saw the van they were in slide over the edge of a mountain pass that had been covered in a slick layer of mud from a recent rainfall. They watched as the van tumbled down the steep, heavily wooded hillside. Moving closer they recognized the people in and outside the vehicle. Ben had been the first to die, being ejected easily from the back seat, he'd hit a tree hard, falling to the ground and being impaled by a sharp, jagged edge of a broken tree limb. Sandra, Ben and Eric's little sister had died next, her neck breaking as her head slammed against the side of the van as it fell. Their parent's died when the front of the van slammed into the dirt at the end of the fall, their bodies lying limp against the shattered windshield.

Eric, Derek and Kyle had all crawled free from the wreckage. They had stumbled up the hillside, finding Ben's broken body. As the night set in the three friends, each with considerable injuries of their own, slowly succumbed to the rapidly falling temperature. Kyle had been the first to die, his side gashed open and his ribcage crushed. Eric had come next, his badly injured body bleeding internally until he drowned in his own blood. Derek was the last to go. While his injuries weren't life threatening, the fact that he was only wearing jeans and a t-shirt hadn't served him well as the temperatures dropped below freezing as winter finally set in. All seven bodies had been found not too long after that, each carefully removed. The funeral the boys watched had been epic for their small town. Derek saw his family, along with Kyle's. Ben and Eric's extended family had also been in attendance. The boys they'd been wrapped arms around each other's necks, holding tight to the fringes of their existence as it was.

"Well shit," Kyle said, echoing the thoughts of his friends. "I guess we all screwed up, huh?"

"Nah, just a little detour. Who cares if Ben thought he grew up to bang a hot chick named Elizabeth and we all thought we went camping. It could be worse than all of us being dead. We could be alive and hate each other," Derek said, logically.

"So we're going to haunt this place for the rest of existence?" Ben asked, finally convinced of his passing.

"It could be worse." Derek laughed. "I could be like all you douche bags. At least I can imagine getting laid." He turned as Sophia, his hot nurse in training came from the fog. What none of them had expected was for her to offer a hand to each of them.

"You can come with me now. It took considerably longer than I had originally thought, but now that you are finally able to know and accept your deaths the way they truly happened, it's time to go."

The boys all followed the beautiful young woman into the fog. Ben looked back as the fog created a thick wall, firmly blocking off the land of the living. As they continued to walk each boy picked up screams of torment. "Where are we going?" Ben asked, noticing how the fog had turned to a deep red color and seemed to be flow-ing thicker, like a river now instead of wispy fog.

"You'll see Benjamin. You and all your friends are in for a rare treat indeed. So many young people end up going the other way, such is the innocence of youth. You four, though, hmm, so carnal in your thinking and actions. Little devils you are. Your paradise will look a little dif-ferent."

"Like what?" Derek asked, smacking her bottom with his hand.

"You like that don't you, Derek?" the young woman asked. As Derek started to answer though, the woman changed right before their eyes. Eric, Ben and Kyle started to back up; hoping to head back the way the girl had brought them. Turning all four boys saw what the woman had truly been. With burning red eyes, glistening fangs and massive muscles, the four friends saw a de-mon in the woman's place.

"Well come on then, bring it on boys. After all, if it's carnal in nature, Hell is certainly the place to see it ful-filled. So grab on Derek and I'll take you for a ride you'll never forget."

All four boys screamed as the floor fell out from under their feet. As their bodies fell through the levels of Hell, the screamed pierced their minds, imbedding them with flashes of pain and horrible, horrible images. The lives of other people who'd died horrible deaths at the hands of others, or hadn't believed enough in the after life to make a different choice.

When they finally landed they were thrown into cages, awaiting a fate that was beyond anything they would've wished on their worst enemies. And the screams continued, ripping through what was left of their souls.

***

Derek bolted upright in the tent, his eyes meeting the terrified faces of his three friends as they also woke to greet November 1st.

Dead Times

Jake Turner slowly registered the incessant beeping of his alarm. Rolling over with a groan he managed to hit the snooze button, knocking the alarm off his bedside table. Rolling back over and flopping an arm over his eyes, Jake wondered if getting out of bed was really worth it. This last week had been like living through the seventh circle of hell, only without the unending fire and brimstone bullshit. Finally tossing back the covers, Jake crawled into the shower with the sluggish motivation of a sloth. An hour later though, he was dressed in his finest suit and ready to face whatever the day brought.

Descending the stairs, Jake hit the button on his coffeemaker, listening as the percolation process started. Knowing he was tight on time, Jake popped two pastries into the toaster and depressed the button. As soon as the coffee was done, he poured some into his thermos, gave it a good shake to mix up the sugar and creamer, and headed out the door as the first rays of sun were streaming across the sky.

Jake waved to his neighbors without looking up at them, such was their routine. He knew they'd be out grabbing the morning paper, just as they knew he'd be rushing to work. Just another routine day in Jake's boring-as-hell life. Jake noticed that there weren't nearly as many cars on the road that morning, which was odd to say the least. Shrugging it off, he continued on towards the office. Merging onto the interstate was a breeze as Jake noticed again that no one seemed to be driving. **What the hell was going on?** Jake wondered. Turning on the radio, Jake scanned the stations until he found a news source.

This is an emergency bulletin for all residents in the tri-state area. Stay indoors. Keep your windows and doors locked and do not, for any reason go outside. There is a contagion in the air making people sick. Again, I repeat. Stay indoors. If you hear anyone telling you it's safe, don't believe them. It is not safe outside. Do not go outside unless it is an absolute life and death emergency. This message will repeat every fifteen minutes. For more information tune to channel 950AM.

Jake immediately flipped to the given channel.

Given the nature and severity of this issue, we are advising people to stock up. Food, water, non-perishables, first aid items; anything that will be useful over the coming weeks, people need to get in order. We advise people not go out on their own. Whatever this disease is it's spreading rapidly. The sick are mobile and for whatever reason they are targeting other civilians. We can't keep a lid on this any longer. Stay inside as long as possible. Gather as much food and water as you can, but never, never go out alone. If you feel sick, quarantine yourself. From the little we know of the disease, the onset happens at death, so it's likely that you won't catch it through the air or body fluid or human contact. Do not let any of the sick into your home. Those who are sick are targeting healthy humans. You must not feel sorry for them. There is literally nothing that can be done to save them. Keep yourself and loved ones safe, that is how you can help the ones who are already suffering the ravages of the disease. If you don't have a safe place to stay, come to 1217 N. Lincoln Ave. Ring the buzzer twice, wait five seconds and ring it again. We'll take as many people as we can. Be strong America. This message will repeat every ten minutes.

What sort of disease were they talking about that would make sick people target other humans to make them sick? Shaking his head Jake continued toward work. With less than ten minutes to go on his commute Jake entered the city limits. He slowed down when he saw that literally no one was on the street. *What the hell?* Paper littered the street and cars were parked every which way, some even driven onto the sidewalk. Ambulances, fire trucks and trash trucks some with their lights still running, were just sitting in the street, unattended. Taking out his cell phone, Jake called his ex-wife, Stacey. Hearing the familiar beep indicating

75

no signal, Jake cursed, shoving his phone into his brief-case. Jake parked in the parking garage on the B level, which he always did. He took out his pass card and grabbing his briefcase, stepped from his car.

He pushed the button for the elevator, whistling while he waited for it to ding. It opened relatively quickly, es-pecially for a Tuesday. Checking his watch, Jake stepped into the elevator, noticing for the first time the other people in the box with him. "Morning." Jake said with a pleasant if dismissive smile.

"Morning." the couple said in unison. Jake wasn't posi-tive they were a couple, but their body language said they were. The woman was turned toward the man, whose arm was around her waist. "Crazy out there isn't it?"

"Yeah. I hardly saw any traffic coming into town and the streets, what the hell's going on?"

"Don't know. We heard some weird news bulletin on the radio, but no one seems to know what this disease is, how it spreads or where the infected people are."

"Let's hope Mr. Moseley didn't get it. He's horrible enough as it is." the man said.

"Absolutely." Jake agreed. "So you work in the same building as me?"

"Yeah. I'm on the fourth floor, accounting department." the man said with a grin. "If there's one thing I do understand, it's money."

"Right." Jake replied. "I'm on the top floor, lawyer."

"How do you deal with him day in and day out man?"

"I've been married and divorced twice. Mr. Moseley has nothing on my ex-wives. If I learned anything from them it was passive interaction. You smile and shake your head and say **ugh-huh** every now and then. They assume you're listening and when they get done with their spiel, you go on about your business."

"Ha!" the man laughed. His woman didn't look too pleased with the advice, but Jake figured it'd be cruel to not clue the man in now. "I'll be damned. I'm gonna have to use that tactic the next time he does his corporate meeting bullshit. The only reason I go to those is because they pay us and the mini-vacation is nice. Other than that, they can stuff the meetings and the **let's do what's best for the company** bullshit."

"And don't you just love his line about how every employee contributes to lasting success?" Jake added.

"Please, the only thing lasting about this company is its CEO."

"Right." Jake agreed. "Well this is your stop. I'll talk to you later."

"Sounds good." the man said. "I'm Eli by the way. Eli Bradford."

"Nice to meet you Eli. I'm Jake Turner." Jake replied, giving a light wave as the doors to the elevator shut. Jake continued up to the second floor, automatically re-adjusting his tie as he went. Stepping off the elevator, Jake knew something was wrong. No one was at registration and there was no sign of the usual life that flowed through the office. In fact, there the only thing Jake did notice, was the silence. **Complete and utter silence**, Jake thought as he roamed the halls looking for anyone who might know what the hell was going on.

"Hello?" Jake called, listening to the echo as it bounced off the walls. Turning Jake thought he heard a noise over by the break room. Heading that way, Jake caught sight of a man who looked as if acid had been poured over his face. "Sir?"

"Uuuugggghhhhh." the man gargled.

"Sir, Do you need help?" Jake asked, clearly not getting through to the man. Dressed in a suit that looked old and torn with dirt stains caking the fabric, Jake thought he looked like he'd dug his way out of a grave. Looking closer at the man's face, Jake gasped. One of the man's eyes was bloodied to the point that Jake was sure he'd lose it if he didn't get to an emergency room. The other eye seemed unable to focus, shooting from one direction to the other and back again. When the man snarled at Jake his teeth looked as if they were rotting out of his mouth, chipped and broken, the man certainly could have used a dentist. Leaving the man, who couldn't seem to care less about his help, Jake wandered through the rest of the office looking for anyone else who may be there. Walking down a long hallway, Jake once again heard the garbled sound of movement.

Turning the corner he saw a woman whose business suit was dirty and ripped, as if she'd crawled over broken glass at some point. She looked at Jake and snarled, much like the man had. Her hair was disheveled to say the least and her face and body were marred by scratches that looked infected and festered. "Ma'am, can you tell me what's happening?" Jake asked, but the woman seemed intent on coming after him, not answering his questions. Backing up Jake turned to head back down the hallway, only to find that the man he'd seen earlier was blocking his path. Turning back around, Jake saw the woman had made considerable progress toward him and was now blocking his path that way as well.

"I don't want to hurt you," Jake called to the man, who just kept on coming. The man drew closer, his face in a snarl that had Jake's stomach turning. Seeing no other options, Jake took his briefcase and shoved it into the man's chest, pushing him back. The man just kept coming. Closing his eyes Jake smashed his brief case into the man's face. When the man seemed unfazed by that, Jake hit him again, then again and again until the man fell down. Turning, Jake saw the woman trip over the man, crawl past him and keep coming at him.

"What the hell!" Jake yelled. Turning, Jake ran down the hall toward the elevator. Pressing the button repeatedly Jake bounced on the pads of his feet, waiting for the elevator to come up. Just as he hit the button for the fourth floor, Jake saw the woman heading towards him at a considerable pace for someone who looked as if she wanted to bite him. The doors shut tight and Jake felt the elevator shift to head down.

"Eli!" Jake called, "Eli Bradford!"

"Run!" Jake heard Eli yell. He saw Eli with his girlfriend close on his heels.

"Come on!" Jake called holding the elevator door. Eli made it first, reaching back for his woman.

"Oh shit!" Eli said, pulling his girlfriend into a tight hug. "Holy hell! What the fuck is going on?"

"I don't know, but we need to find out." Jake said. "The bulletins I heard coming into the city said that people were sick with some sort of disease. But the disease isn't airborne and isn't spread through normal channels of human contact. It doesn't have a given incubation period. The people I ran into that looked sick. Christ, they looked like they wanted to bite me."

"Us too." Eli said shaking his head in understanding. "At first all I noticed is that no one seemed to be working. Then I heard Whitney, this is Whitney by the way.

80

Anyway I heard her scream. I come around the corner and see this man, if you could even call him that, trying to bite her. He's snarling and got his filthy hands on her. I hit him in the head and he let her go, then we ran. Not too long after that we heard you call."

"I had a similar experience." Jake affirmed. "Ran into a guy who looked as if he was in desperate need of a shower and a dentist. The woman I saw looked as if she'd been scraped by shards of glass, her face and arms were all cut up, but even then she just kept coming, as if her only objective was to bite me. I'm on B Level, where are you?"

"We're on B too." Eli said, "Where are you headed?"

"Home I guess. I need to see what sort of supplies I have to wait this thing out."

"We're in an apartment on Fifth. Do you want to come with us, or do you mind if we follow you? I don't like the idea of this disease spreading." Eli said, not feeling too concerned about his ego at the moment.

"Me either." Jake said with a shake of his head. "Tell you what, I'll follow you to your apartment. Grab some clothes and all the food and water you can find. Then we'll head out to my place. It seems to me that the country might have a lot less people affected by this than the city. We'll stick together and wait this shit out."

"Sounds good." Eli said. Jake found his car quickly, moving around in the direction Eli and Whitney had headed. He saw them pulling out of their parking space in a newer Nissan. The ten minute drive took them twenty as they maneuvered around abandoned vehicles. Jake followed his two new friends up to their apartment. Thankfully they didn't run into any of the sick on their way. While the two packed their clothes in luggage cases, Jake pulled canned food and water bottles from the cupboards and fridge. He poured ice into a cooler and put the meat from their freezer in it. "We ready to go?"

"Looks like it to me." Jake said, scanning their living room. "It's a nice place you have here." Jake commented as they headed for the door.

"Yeah it was." Eli said, a note of sadness in his voice. "Hopefully one day we'll be able to come back to it. Last minute Eli reached up on the wall and grabbed a photo of an older woman and man in embrace. "My parents." Eli explained. Jake shook his head, leading the way out of the building with the cooler in hand. They made it back to the Nissan and Jake's Chevy. They loaded the luggage and cooler into Eli and Whitney's car and Jake waited for them to get started before moving onto the interstate and showing them the way home.

By nightfall Jake felt pretty secure. The power was out, but Jake used his fireplace to cook a chicken rotisserie style. It was a meager meal, but the three new roommates were full and comfortable. Jake wasn't so sure he could say that about others near his home. Saying goodnight to Eli and Whitney, Jake headed for his bed-room. He'd given the farthest spare bedroom to his new friends, hoping that if they felt the urge to be intimate they'd keep it down to a minimum. Jake knew that rarely did something inspire people to have sex like the end of the world as they knew it.

The early morning hours caught Jake tossing and turn-ing. He hadn't slept well at all, and as he rubbed the grit from his eyes, he noticed that the sun was just peeking over the horizon. Grabbing his cell phone off the coun-ter Jake tried to get a signal again. "Damn it!" Jake cussed. There wouldn't be any calling out today. He headed down stairs in his pajama bottoms, smelling cof-fee and bacon frying.

"Morning," Whitney said. "We thought we'd make breakfast, since you're putting us up and all."

"Thank you." Jake said, taking a cup of coffee from her. "But to make things clear, we're in this together. We eat together, work together and don't go outside alone, at all if we can avoid it."

"You don't have to tell us twice." Eli agreed. "Those things, whatever they were, weren't human. I've heard of cannibals before, but they...." Eli stammered, unable to completely keep his composure.

"They seemed hell-bent on biting us, turning us into one of them." Whitney finished for him, her eyes wor-ried.

"Then we have to make sure they don't get in here. I want to see if there's any wood in the shed. I want to board up as many of these windows as we can. If they want in, we'll at least know they're coming."

"I'll go with you."

"No, you stay with Whitney. If I don't come back in fifteen minutes, you stay inside, no matter what."

"No. You said we shouldn't go out alone, so, since there's only three of us, we all go. We'll get the shit we need, get these windows done and get our asses back inside." Whitney said, all business now.

"She makes the most sense. We don't have enough of us to split up, so we all go together." Eli said. He could tell Jake didn't like the idea, but no one was play hero today.

***

It took them nearly an hour to screw the boards over the windows, but when they were done all the first floor windows were covered. Whitney headed in first, lighting candles that she'd found in a cupboard of miscellaneous items. Eli and Jake worked to stack firewood near the front door for the coming night. It wasn't freezing outside yet, but with fall in full swing the fire would do more than just cook their food. It provided heat and light just in case the candles went out during the night.

At any rate Jake knew it was only a matter of time before the candles would be useless.

He helped Eli and Whitney grind steak into hamburger for burgers that would rival the best burger ever made. Before the week was out, Jake, Eli and Whitney grew used to eating one big meal a day and grazing during their waking hours. What they hadn't grown used to was the sounds they heard outside. Looking through the upstairs windows, they saw what the disease was doing to people. Roaming the streets all hours of the day and night seeking God only knew what as they went. Seemingly brainless, the walking were awake, but Jake doubted they were alive.

"We have to leave." Jake announced five days after meeting Eli and Whitney. "We're out of food after tonight and we can either leave to find more, and maybe come back here, or we'll stay inside here and starve to death."

"Well those are some damn fine choices aren't they?" Eli said, frustrated. "Go out there among those things and hope they don't want to eat us, hope to find food and hope when we come back that this place isn't overrun. Or, we stay and starve. Fuck!"

"Look, no one likes this. I certainly didn't think I'd end up doing this when I went to work Monday. I was dressed in a suit like I did every day. I was ready to tackle cases, not some walking breathing carcass with nasty teeth and a bad case of cannibalistic munchies. But I don't want to do this alone. I know all of us are better off if we stick together." Jake reasoned. "Either of you ever fire a gun before? I know it's a scary prospect, having to shoot one of those things, but we can't think of them as human. Either of you ever run into a rational, living human that wanted to eat you? We think of them as the enemy, pure and simple. It seems to me that being prepared, equipped is the best route of precaution to take. There's a pawn shop three blocks from here that I know had guns and ammo." Jake continued, drawing a map on his living room floor. The grocery is five more blocks this way. If there's any chance of finding food, it'll be there. If that's empty I say we start looking in houses. I know from watching them that my neighbors fell to the disease. I would have known all this early if I'd looked up when I waved at them on Monday."

"Alright, so our plan is to hit the pawn shop, then the grocery store. Then we hit homes if it turns up empty. You have anything in here or the shed we can use as weapons until we get to the pawn shop?"

"Ugh, yeah. I know I've got a machete and a pitch fork in the shed. I also have a chainsaw, and a shovel." Jake said, standing.

"We need to get going then, so we can make it back before dark." Whitney chimed in. "I'm taking the two flares we brought from our emergency road kit. Someone remind me to grab some lighters from the grocery store."

Whitney headed out right behind Eli who took the lead to the shed. She grabbed the shovel, while Eli took the pitchfork and Jake the machete. He looked able to wield it, Whitney thought, looking at Jake. He wasn't as hot as Eli in her eyes, but he had some killer instincts, liked to stay alive at least. She figured they could have found anyone, but she was thankful it was Jake who'd come along to save them.

"Let's head out." Jake said, noticing the four walking people hanging around his driveway. "If they come at you, hit them anywhere you can. Remember, they're the enemy. They aren't people anymore."

Whitney stayed between Jake and Eli, feeling more secure that way. She knew it was weak of her to think so, but she liked having a man on either side of her. The first walking person they ran into Jake hit in the head with the machete. The creeper, as Whitney referred to them, dropped to the ground. Eli took the next one skewering it with the steel tines of the pitchfork. He yanked the pitchfork out of the woman's stomach, but she kept coming at him. Taking matters into her own hands, when Eli stuck her again, Whitney hit the woman in the head. As thick, dark blood pooled around her head, Eli removed the pitchfork. The woman didn't move.

"I think we have to hit them in the head. Eli stuck her twice with that pitchfork and she just kept coming."

"You may be right." Jake said as they continued on. "Let's avoid them if we can, but if not, hit them in the head. We'll waste less energy that way than trying to take them out by stabbing them five or six times each. From what we've seen they move slower than we do, but a mass of them could get sticky real fast. They only have one agenda. We need to survive, that's our agenda."

They hit the pawn shop, perusing the guns that hadn't been pilfered yet. Jake took a sixteen round 9mm, filling the magazine and a spare with ammo. He tucked the ten remaining boxes of ammo into the backpack Whitney had been smart enough to bring along. Eli managed to snag a 12 gauge shotgun that he quickly loaded. He also grabbed the five boxes of shotgun shells, tucking them into the backpack as well. Whitney grabbed a whetstone for sharpening the machete and a sheath she found on the wall. Sliding the machete into the sleeve, she slung the blade over her shoulder. As a precaution she took a .38 revolver, loaded the six rounds it would hold and took the fifteen boxes of ammo to accompany their tiny stash. Then, popping a complimentary mint into her mouth. "I honestly never saw this coming when we went to work on Monday."

"Me either." Eli said, looking out the window of the store. "We need to hurry if we're going to make the grocery store and get back before sunset.

The grocery store proved to be a major letdown. The shelves were virtually wiped clean and what food that was left needed to be cooked with ingredients that wouldn't be easy to use. Eli found three containers of shelf stable milk that would come in handy. Whitney, like any normal, rational thinking woman, raided the candy aisle, grabbing, chocolate covered pretzels, chocolate bars, and pretty much anything that wasn't nailed down. Jake pored over the canned section, picking up anything he thought might be good for eating. With their backpack and two reusable store bags packed full, the three situational friends headed out. "Sun's starting to set, let's move."

"Right behind you." Jake said, carrying one of the bags. Whitney followed Eli, the backpack slung over her slender shoulders. Running along the sidewalk, Jake took a creeper out with a shot to the head. The next one Eli nailed with the butt of his shotgun, shattering his apparently fragile skull. "Eli look out!"

Eli heard Jake's call as if someone had flooded his ears with water, or like he was driving through a tunnel. Turning Eli saw a creeper snarling in his face. Before he could duck out of the way, the creeper lunged, his teeth sinking into Eli's shoulder. "Ah!" Eli screamed, his flesh tearing beneath the clamp-like jaws of the thing that had once been human. "Go!"

Jake stopped next to Eli, whose arm was now useless, blood soaked his shirt, oozing from an artery that had been torn by pointed, razor sharp teeth. "Shit." Jake cussed. Looking at Eli, Jake saw the loss of blood was taking it's toll. Even if the creepers didn't finish him off, there was no way Eli was walking with them for long. Pointing his pistol at the creeper's head, Jake turned his face and pulled the trigger. The creepers jaw let go and Jake grabbed Eli's arm, pulling him along with them. "We're not leaving you behind."

"You might as well. Didn't you hear the bulletin? It's not airborne and isn't spread through normal human contact. It's the bite that kills you Jake. Once you're bitten there's no hope of surviving the disease. If they don't kill me, I'll die anyway. Then, when I awaken like them, I'll be a mortal danger to you and Whitney. I won't go Jake." Eli proclaimed. "I won't chance that I might hurt either of you, especially the woman I love."

"There has to be a way." Jake insisted angrily. "You can't believe everything you hear on the news you know."

"Maybe not, but I believe they were telling the truth and if the burn in this wound says anything, it's that the disease is already pumping hot through my system. I won't have long before the infection changes me into a creeper and what I was won't be what I become. I'd spare both of you from that."

"Eli..." Whitney said, pulling him into a hug. "Please."

"Whit, we talked about this. We talked about what we'd do if this happened. We agreed that we'd want all our memories to be good ones. I don't want you to see me like them. I want you to remember our trip to Rio. I want you to remember the night I asked you to marry me. I want you to know beyond a shadow of a doubt that I loved you. I won't smudge those memories by turning into one of them in front of you. I won't have either of you ending me to save yourself. Now go before more of them come. It looks like noise attracts them."

"Eli…" Jake started.

"I said go!" Eli shouted, tears springing to his eyes. He pulled Whitney into his arms, kissing her deeply before pulling away and pushing her away from him. "Take care of her Jake. Please, from one human to another. Don't let her become like them." He tossed Jake his shotgun and turning around, walked toward the creepers.

"Eli!" Whitney screamed, beating Jake's chest as he held her back. "Eli please!"

"We have to go now Whitney. Come on." Jake soothed. Neither Whitney, nor Jake mentioned how it had turned their stomachs to hear Eli's screams as the creepers attacked him. Neither of them mentioned how they'd never forget the sound. The last two blocks home were fast, silent. Jake ushered Whitney into the house just as the last rays of sunlight filtered across the sky.

"Screw you, Jake!" Whitney said, turning on Jake the moment they were both inside. "We could have saved him!" She beat on his chest again, her angry arms flailing to relieve the grief in her heart.

"You know better than that," Jake said, gripping her wrists tight, until she could no longer move her arms. "Look at me. You know better than that Whitney. We couldn't have saved him. He knew it and did exactly what you would have done if it was you. He wanted you safe and the best way to do that was for us to be away from him."

The tears came now, hot, furious, heavy. They soaked through Jake's shirt as Whitney sobbed, sagging against him until Jake had to hold her up. Sitting down on the couch in his living room, Jake held Whitney like a child until her sobbing finally slowed. When she fell asleep he eased her down onto the sofa, slowly slipping from under her legs. He put the canned food in the cupboards and worked to light the fire, pulling an afghan over Whitney's shoulders. Outside, Jake heard the unending noise of the growing mass of creepers lurking around, waiting for any opening to snack on the closest living human.

***

It didn't take long for the general populace that was left to realize the government's hand in creating the outbreak that everyone had labeled "The Disease." Government agencies from the CIA to the FBI and NSA, all blamed one another for cover-ups, conspiracies, back door deals and lobbying nightmares that resulted in the craziness that had been witnessed by every class of people. Rich, poor, white, black, Asian, Indian, Native American, it didn't matter the color or creed of your people. Realizing that the experiment had gotten out of control, the government had shut it's doors, declaring a state of national emergency and hiding in the military grade bunkers of the Cold War era, they thought to wait the disease out, hoping it'd eventually wear off.

Jake and Whitney learned to survive. They built a small memorial to Eli and moved on. Eventually they'd had to leave their safe house, knowing that food and clean water would only become more and more scarce and the time went on. As horrid times usually do, Jake and Whitney were drawn together as well, finding comfort in each other where they couldn't find it anywhere else. The disease ravaged the best of people and made it easy to bring out the worst. Jake and Whitney found out the hard way more than once, coming upon people who'd turned to cannibalism and heinous acts to "stay alive." Riding through a forested area, Whitney was nearly beheaded by a chain that had been stretched across some trees. Jake had fought normal humans to keep them from taking her, their evil intents clear in the laughing sneers they gave her. Any sense of normalcy had long since disappeared.

***

Whitney tucked the journal into her jacket and picked up a few other things. Turning she looked at Jake. It'd been a while now since they'd truly communicated. Jake had been attacked three weeks earlier, by a crowd of creepers. Whitney had objected to him going out of the house alone, but he'd been adamant. By the time she'd saved him nearly all of his face, where the first bite had occurred had been badly mangled. Flesh hung in huge, grotesquely torn pieces. Part of his neck flesh was missing and other important organs had taken a beating. Still, Whitney had killed the creepers close to him.

Knowing he'd turn quickly, Whitney had taken action, chaining Jake's hands together to a post and using the machete, hacking his jaw so that it hung from the hinged muscles, useless. After that he'd been like a pet. He followed her wherever she went, content to gargle continuously and keep Whitney relatively safe.

They'd learned within their first week of being outside the safe house that if staying alive was their main objective, and really what could be of higher priority than that, they had to look and smell like other creepers. Whitney smirked, remembering how she'd vomited from the rank smell of death that clung to her skin and clothes. She had killed a creeper and painted her face and clothes with the man's organs. It wouldn't be the last time she'd had to do it, unfortunately, Whitney thought.

When he woke, which Whitney knew by then, wouldn't take but a few minutes, she was ready. Cuffing his wrists to a rope, Whitney kept Jake with her. The first time she went into other overrun facilities, it didn't take long for

Whitney to realize the creepers didn't bother her. Between her disgusting clothes and Jake tied to her, they simply didn't see or smell her. She found an amazing medical bag that fit like a back pack. It had been tucked into a cabinet that by some miracle hadn't been pilfered. It became her carry all bag for anything she deemed worthy enough.

Rifling through a library, Whitney had found a first edition copy of **Hamlet** she tucked away for posterity, or burning if she was desperate for a fire. She also grabbed Steinbeck's **The Grapes of Wrath**, simply because she liked the story and she sort of felt like Tom Joad. While she technically had never killed someone, taking out the creepers wasn't far from it. Not to mention the journey she'd been on since Jake found her and Eli.

Whitney stared down the highway that would lead her into her future, as bleak as that thought was. Tugging Jake's rope, she straightened her shoulders and started walking. Only time would tell whether she was walking toward something, or away from it.

Welcome Home

Beginnings

Sandra Setterington pulled up to the huge, dilapidated house and put her road weary station wagon in park. Her girls were sleeping, which Sandra saw as a blessing. Leaving them be, she climbed the wide front porch steps, noticing how they sagged under her weight, which wasn't impressive to say the least. Always slender, she'd never been one to pack the pounds on. The fact that the steps were already weak meant that she'd spend a considerable amount of time fixing them. She put her key in the lock and turned it, hearing the screeching click of the lock. Sandra opened the door wide, covering her mouth against the plume of dust that billowed out toward her. Stepping into the foyer of the old mansion, Sandra looked up as sun streamed in through the windows.

"First things first," Sandra muttered to herself. Pulling her long brown hair back into a ponytail, she set to work yanking down the tattered curtains that haphazardly covered the stained and broken windows.

"Morning!" a voice called from the porch. Sandra looked through the smudged glass noticing the stranger. Moving to the doorway, she was able to get a better look at the man. He was rugged, broad in his shoulders with large hands that looked as if they knew their way around a tool shed and a hard day's work. "I'm Nick Driscoll."

Sandra looked at his outstretched hand. Slowly she stepped onto the porch. "Nice to meet you Mr. Driscoll. I'm Sandra," Sandra returned, extending her own hand. Just then Sandra looked toward her car where her girls were waking up.

"Mama!" little Annie called.

"I'm here girls!" Sandra called back. "Excuse me Mr. Driscoll, I have to see to my children."

"No problem," the man replied.

Sandra made herself concentrate on her daughter's, resisting the strong urge to look back at the captivating man. "Is this our new home mama?"

"It sure is, girls. We've got a lot of work to do to get it ready to live in though. Are you girls hungry?"

"Yes," the two girls chimed in unison. Sandra smiled, reaching in her pack to pull out two juice boxes and two cinnamon rolls. It wasn't the breakfast of champions, but it'd serve them well until she could go shopping. Sandra turned toward the house, seeing that Mr. Driscoll was still on her porch.

"Mr. Driscoll, these are my daughters, Annie and Jaime. Girls, this is Mr. Driscoll. He's our neighbor."

They smiled, waving.

***

Nick watched the woman with her two little girls. They favored her, although the older girl had nearly white blonde hair that curled at the ends. The woman, Sandra, was tall and lean. Nick couldn't dismiss her beauty, though. She had curves in places every woman should. He couldn't guess her age, but from the look of her body, Nick assumed she was probably in her late twenties or early thirties. She looked as if she took good care of her body and if the steely determination in her eyes said anything to Nick it was that she'd had to fight for what she had and she'd fight tooth and nail to keep it. Nick liked that.

"I had heard that someone had bought this old place. Never imagined anyone would want to fix it up, though," Nick said, looking from the old house to Sandra.

"I wanted a place my girls could feel free. I didn't have a lot of money to work with, but this house will look amazing when I'm done with it," Sandra explained, the steely determination was back.

"Well, I have a fair hand with carpentry and I'm not afraid of an honest days work. I'd only be free weeknights and on Saturday, but if you find yourself in need I'm available," Nick said, tucking his business card into a splinter in one of the porch columns. "I wrote my personal phone number on the back of the card. You should be able to reach my anytime, if the need arises."

"Thank you Mr. Driscoll."

"Please, call me Nick," the man insisted.

"Alright, Nick," Sandra returned. "If you're free now, I was going to start taking stock of the house and what I'll need to replace. I'm thinking about scrapping all the windows and ordering a whole new set, but I'm not sure that's the most economical decision."

Nick looked at the windows. "Let's get them cleaned up and then I can give you better advice on whether or not the full windows need to be replaced."

"I'd appreciate that," Sandra replied. She returned to her car and pulled out all her cleaning supplies. They worked into the early evening, stopping only long enough to eat a meager lunch. The girls ran around the house, playing and arguing over which room belonged to which girl. Jaime claimed the larger of the two smaller rooms and both girls exclaimed over the room that would be their mother's.

"It's huge mama!" little Annie said with an exaggerated gasp.

"It is. I guess I'll have to find some cheap furniture to fill all the space up huh?" Sandra smiled, picking her youngest girl up for a tickle. Annie squealed and ran around again as soon as Sandra put her feet on the floor.

"They're great kids," Nick commented, spraying down the windows on the far side of the room. Both adults made sure to never be in the same room together alone. Nick wasn't sure how Sandra felt, but if the tension between them said anything, he was certain she was just as anxiously uncomfortable as he was.

Dinner was light, thanks to Nick. He ordered pizza and added soda and ice cream to treat the girls. "Thanks Mr. Nick!" Annie and Jaime both squealed when they saw the ice cream.
"Thank you, Nick." Sandra said, her smile bright and beautiful.

Nick waited for Sandra to tuck the girls into their spots. He listened to her short story, smiling when the girls giggled. "I think they'll sleep for a year," Sandra said as she came back to sit with Nick on the porch.

"Are you sure y'all will be safe out here?"

"I think so." Sandra looked back at the house. The electric would be turned on the following morning and Sandra had taken Nick's advice and using his cell phone, called for an estimate to be made on new windows.

"If you decide to get the windows replaced, let me know. I'll come over and get started on new framing. The new windows will need it."

"Thank you again, Nick, for everything," Sandra said, resting her hand over his and giving it a squeeze. There was a moment when Nick wanted very badly to kiss this woman, whose green eyes shone like beacons, but something shifted in those worried eyes and Nick let the moment pass. Maybe taking it slow wouldn't be such a hardship, he thought. Standing Nick bid Sandra a good night, turning to walk back to his own home.

Friendly Encounters

Sandra woke with the sun, stretching to relieve the sore muscles that had spent a night cramped into her front seat. The girls scrambled around when they woke, running through the house again. She excused the girls to their prospective rooms when the window retail representative came out. Jaime and Annie took off, giggling as they clamored for the big room. Jaime reached it first effectively slamming the door in Annie's face.

"Fine!" the younger girl yelled, stomping off to her own room. Annie closed her own door deciding to sit in the middle of her room. She hummed a few bars of her favorite song and played with her one and only doll.

"That's a pretty doll you have."

Annie looked up at the sound and saw a small girl sitting across from her. "Thank you," Annie replied, a small smile on her face.

"I'm Tiny. My real name is Trisha, but my family calls me Tiny." Annie just stared at the girl for a minute.

"I'm Annie. My mom and sister call me Annie. My doll's name is Corky, because my mom said she's made of cork wood."

"I had a doll once, but I lost her," Tiny said. "Why is your mother cleaning our house?"

"Your house?" Annie asked, confused. "My mom bought it with her monies. She said we could each pick a room of our own!"

"Oh. Well this room is mine and the bigger room belongs to my brother. He's mean to me so I stay away from him, but I heard him telling my mama that you don't belong here," Tiny responded.

"Older brothers and sisters are always mean," Annie said with emphasis. "My older sister took the bigger room, too."

"Who are you talking to?" Jaime asked, sneering.

"Tiny, she's my new friend. She said that you're sleeping in her brother's room and that he said we don't belong here."

"No one's owned this house in forever," Jaime told her, as if she knew everything about everything. "We own it now so *Tiny* can get over it."

"Don't say that!" Annie defended her friend. "Tiny's nice and I like her."

"Whatever," Jaime replied, moving on to find her mother. Jaime saw her mother talking to the window guy and Nick. Jaime wasn't sure how to feel about Nick yet. He seemed nice, but she also knew he looked googly eyed at her mother. No one who did that really cared.

"Annie, Jaime, come down here girls," Sandra called to her girls. Seconds later Annie practically ran Jaime over on her way down the stairs.

"Hey!" Jaime yelled, offended.

"Sorry!" Annie called, "Tiny made me lose my balance." The girls scrambled downstairs, each trying to beat the other. "Hi mom!"

"Hi sweetheart," Sandra said with a chuckle. "Next time try not to knock your sister down the stairs."

"Okay, but it was Tiny's fault." Annie pouted.

"And who's Tiny?"

"Tiny's my friend. I met her up in my room. She has a brother named Jacob and parents too. This is their house. Jacob doesn't want us to be here."

"Well," Sandra exaggerated, "Jacob will just have to learn to live with us then won't he?"

"Tiny said Jacob won't like you saying that."

"She's just being dramatic." Jaime chimed in, standing on the other side of her mother.

"Am not!" Annie retorted.

"Are too!" Jaime shot back.

"Alright girls," Sandra stated firmly. "Jaime, Annie, this is Mr. Nolan. He'll be around for the next few weeks taking a look at our windows and helping us get the framework done right so we can have new windows put in."

"Hello ladies," Mr. Nolan smiled. He was older, but handsome for his age. With silver specks glittering his otherwise dark hair. His eyes were a bright blue that complimented his smile. Jaime wondered if every man was going to give her mother that look. She wasn't sure what it meant exactly, but it seemed that every man she met looked oddly at her mom.

When the man left Jaime asked her mother about it, making sure Nick wasn't anywhere around. "What's that look mean, mom?"

"What look, honey?" Sandra asked, wiping down a mirror that she'd hung on the wall, turning toward Jaime.

"That look that men give you."

"Oh," Sandra replied, understanding. "Well sometimes it just means that they think I'm pretty and appreciate that fact. Sometimes, like with Nick, it means a little more than that."

"So Nick likes you?" Jaime asked, her doe eyes looking a little lost.

"I think so, but there's no rush for that sort of thing. Mommy isn't hurrying into anything except finishing this house up so we have a safe and stable place to live."

"Good," Jaime said, wrapping her arms around her mother's waist. She was gone again, like a shot from a cannon, leaving Sandra to her straightening. Turning around again, Sandra caught her breath. The mirror she'd hung on her bedroom wall was cracked, a spider web design spreading out from a center point of impact.

**

"Everything okay?" Nick asked, standing in the doorway. Sandra turned toward him, those bright green eyes clouded, unsure.

"Yeah," she replied. "I just have to replace this mirror. I hung it up, turned to talk to Jaime and when I turned back it was cracked."

"Ah, people around these parts think this place is haunted, you know?"

"Really?" Sandra questioned. "And what do you think?"

"I've never experienced anything personally, but word has it that there was a family who lived here once upon a time that was murdered. Apparently the father left to find work or some such situation. When he came back he found his wife in bed with someone else. In his rage he hurt her the only way he knew how, by taking the lives of their children. The last couple that bought this place didn't make it more than six months. I stopped by right before they left to see how the renovations were coming. They told me they hadn't been able to get any-thing done because the house wouldn't let them."

"Huh. Do you know where I can find out more infor-mation about the family that was murdered here?"
"Not sure, but it seems like the local library should have something. I've gotta get back into town, I'll stop and see if I can find anything out."

"Thanks," Sandra offered. "I appreciate it and every-thing truly."

"You're very welcome," Nick said, waiting. "Would you, would you and the girls like to go to dinner with me?" Nick watched her closely; those huge green eyes drew to his like a moth to a flame.

"No one's ever asked me out quite like that before," Sandra said softly.

"Well I sort figured you wouldn't want to leave your little ones behind, not to mention who do you really have to watch them?"

"Alright Nick," Sandra agreed with a smile. "We'll join you for dinner. Thank you."

"It's my pleasure Sandra, truly," he replied, tipping his hat, Nick excused himself, saying he'd pick them all up around 6pm.

***

The next week flew by. Nick came out every afternoon to help them work on the house. Jaime decided he wasn't so bad. He played around with them and twice now he'd taken them to dinner. She still wasn't sure about the looks he gave her mama, but Jaime figured if looking at her mama was the payment he got for dinner, it wasn't so bad. Annie adored him, which was natural enough for a girl her age.

She talked constantly about Tiny, Jacob and their family. Sandra had yet to "meet" any of them, but she indulged her daughter as best she could. Sandra had three more mirrors break on her and every time she put the curtains in the house up she'd come downstairs or back from town to see them strewn every which way.

"Tiny says Jacob is angry that we haven't left yet. She said Jacob and their parents want their house back."

"Well you can tell Tiny to tell Jacob and her parents that I'll give them their house back just the way it was. I did some research, thanks to Nick, on the house and its occupants. Then I found some great books on eighteenth century art and architecture. It may take me the rest of my life, but I'm going to make sure this house looks amazing again."

"I'll tell her, but I don't think they'll change their minds," Annie said, her face serious. Sandra chuckled to herself as her daughter headed to her room.

***

"She's doing what she can!" Annie said, her voice earnest. "You have to tell them that we like it here. It's the first real home we've ever had. I don't want to leave!"

"I'll tell them, but they don't listen to what I say. They always say I'm too little to understand."

"Me too," Annie agreed. "Please, you have to try."

"I will. I like having you here, but it won't be easy to tell them."

Tiny vanished and the area where Annie sat grew warm again. She didn't like that it got so cold when Tiny was here, but she did like having a friend who understood her. "Annie." Jacob said, allowing her to see him for the first time. Annie turned around slowly as she'd been heading for her bedroom door.
"Annie I know you like it here and that you've made friends with my sister, but you have to leave. You and your family can't be here."

"Why?" Annie asked, confused.

"Because!" Jacob yelled, causing the door to Annie's room to slam ferociously. "If your family stays here, he'll come back. Don't you understand? He'll come back!"

"Who?" Annie asked, still not understanding.

"Does it matter?" Jacob said, tossing the small toys in Annie's room to and fro. "I said you have to leave!"

"Annie!" Sandra called, banging hard on the bedroom door. "Annie, let me in!"

"You tell your mother that she has to leave this place, or I'll make it painfully clear to her," Jacob threatened. Annie simply nodded, the fear soaking into her skin as she stood there staring. Sandra barreled through the door as if she'd never been shut out. She bumped into Annie who didn't seem to register her presence for a minute.

"Annie?" Sandra said, squatting in front of her daughter. Annie's eyes were glassy as she stared at the wall. Clapping her hands hard in front of Annie's face, Sandra was relieved when the little girl's eyes tracked to her face. "There you are." Sandra pulled her little girl into a hard hug. "What happened in here?"

"I told you Jacob didn't want you here. He said we have to leave or he'll make it painfully clear to you. Jacob said that if we didn't leave, he'd come back."

"Who'd come back, sweetheart?"

"I don't know. But I think Jacob's afraid of him and so am I, now." Annie cried, tears soaking into Sandra's shirt.

"Oh sweetheart," Sandra soothed stroking Annie's long, dark hair. "I think that Tiny and Jacob need to take a break from visiting you for a while. Tonight you'll sleep in my room, you and Jaime."

"Jaime won't like that," Annie said, still pouting.

"No, but she'll survive," Sandra assured her. "How about we go down and order some pizza. We'll rent a movie and make some popcorn too."

"Okay!" Annie squealed, grabbing Sandra's hand and pulling her from the room. That night the girls slept with Sandra in her massive king-sized bed. Tossing and turning Annie crept from the bed, knowing she'd find Tiny up and roaming. "I knew you'd be here."

"I can't sleep. Never do we sleep at night. I swear its part of our restlessness or something," Tiny said, her dark eyes twinkling in the moonlight. Jacob says it's because when we died we had unfinished business. I think it's because I wanted a treat before bed when I died. My father had promised me one, but he didn't give it to me. Then I died."

"I'm sorry," Annie told her, truly feeling for her friend. "I like treats, too. Mama made us popcorn tonight and we got to watch Transylvania!"

"Oh I like that place. I haven't been yet, but I hope to go there some day."

"You can go places?" Annie asked, curious now.

"Sure. Although it takes a lot of energy conversion for that distance. Jacob says I'll never be able to go because I'm too small. I can't convert energy the way he and my parents can."

"I thought I told you not to talk to her!" Jacob growled, grabbing Tiny by the arm. She screamed, piercing Annie's ears with the abnormally high-pitched tone. Annie covered her ears, dropping to the floor. "Didn't I tell you to talk to your mother?"

"I did!" Annie defended herself. "I told her we had to leave. She said we were staying and that eventually you'd grow to like what we were doing with the place."

"Fine, bitch doesn't want to listen," Jacob spat. Moving past Annie with frigid, angry strides; Jacob climbed onto the bed. Straddling Sandra, Jacob brought his face within inches of Sandra's, letting the frosty air coat her body until she started to shiver. "Get out, bitch!"

Sandra felt as if someone had frozen her bones and then placed them in her body. She hadn't expected it to get so cold this early in the year. Tossing, she tried to get warm without disturbing the girls. Bolting upright in bed Sandra felt as if her heart would simply fall from her chest. Her ears were ringing and her pulse was pounding. As the cold air dissipated, Sandra looked up to see Annie standing in the sitting area of her bedroom, her eyes pouring tears as she trembled.

"Come here, sweetheart," Sandra called softly, holding out her arms. "Come and get warm with mommy."

"I told you they want us to leave." Annie wailed. She sobbed in her mother's arms for more than an hour before Sandra was able to soothe her to sleep. Sandra slept fitfully as well, her own system on alert for what, she had no idea.

***

He watched them now, sleeping soundly in their big bed. It'd been forever it felt like, since anyone had actually stayed. He couldn't blame people really. Ghosts were scary and the one's that haunted this house were right up there with poltergeists. Still the smoking hot mother and her two precious girls were sticking it out. He had no doubt that something was brewing. He heard enough during the day and at night to know that the resident ghosts weren't happy with their new house-mates. Broken mirrors, torn up curtains, the littlest girl being scared out of her mind.

Smiling, he sat his binoculars down and took a sip of his hot coffee, nothing like caffeine to jump start the system. It wouldn't be long now. A few more months and they'd either leave, or disappear. Both had happened before and one or the other would happen again. It wasn't that he liked being right, but there was a certain righteousness that came with the knowing of fact. And for the mother and her two girls, it was a fact that they'd leave; one way or another.

Putting his binoculars and other tools away, the stranger put his things away and walked calmly to his truck, whistling a very happy tune. For someone who had no good in him, he was very, very happy.

Revelations

Sandra used a large roller to spread tacky glue over the wall's surface while Nick laid down new wallpaper in the foyer. The last two weeks had made an impressive difference in the look and feel of the house. Thanks in large part to Nick, the new windows had been put in and with the furnace and air conditioning system getting an upgrade, Sandra was able to start furnishing the home she couldn't wait to truly call **home**. "It looks good right?" Sandra asked Nick as they finished the last strip.

"Yeah," Nick replied, wrapping an arm around Sandra's waist. "It looks amazing."

"I certainly think so." Sandra smiled. She turned when she heard Jaime and Annie coming down the stairs. Jaime reached her first as usual, but when Sandra looked up to see Annie, she nearly fainted. The little girl coming down the stairs was not Annie. Her hair was too light, closer to Jaime's color than Annie's. Her freckles were too persistent too, splaying over her entire face, where Annie's was just a smattering across her nose. "Annie?"

"Hello, Mrs. Setterington. Annie is fine. Jacob thought it'd be best if I came to talk to you in person, so I used Annie's body to do that. She's sleeping right now, but Jacob's watching over her so she'll be alright."

"Oh god," Sandra whispered, sitting on the bottom step of the steps. "What did you need to talk to me about and you are you?"

"I'm Tiny. Well my real name is Trisha Meers, but my family calls me Tiny." Sandra's face went nearly white. She knew the Meers name. They'd owned the house and were the family that had been murdered within the four walls of the home. The mother and father had been found in the bed, naked, their bodies still intimately embraced. The boy had been killed in the bathroom, his body naked as well. The little girl, Trisha, had been smothered in her bed.

"Trisha, why is it that your family doesn't want us to live here?" Sandra asked, her voice shaking violently.

"Because. Jacob thinks that man who did this will come back again if you don't leave," Tiny explained. "Whenever someone buys this house, the man who killed us comes back. He watches at first, makes notes, plans, and plans for his plans. If the family isn't scared enough of us, he takes other measures to ensure they leave the house alone. This time it's different, though. He likes the look of you and thinks you will look good here, you and your children."

"He who?" Sandra asked. She watched as Trisha lifted her hand and pointed a finger toward the doorway. When Sandra followed that pointing finger though it was like being slammed into the Twilight Zone. Trisha was pointing at Nick, but it wasn't Nick that Sandra saw anymore.

"He can hurt you, Mrs. Setterington. He uses other people's bodies to do his bidding. Be careful." Before Sandra could look, little Trisha was gone and Annie lay next to her, resting peacefully, as if she'd chosen to curl up on the stairs to nap.

"Hello, Sandra," the man she knew as Nick said. His voice was different now though and his mannerisms had changed, too.

"Who are you?"

"Well that'd depend on who you asked. Little Trisha didn't know the real me in life. I didn't know either of my lover's children. I did know her massive dick of a husband, though. You see, Beatrice and I were meant to be. I was crazy about her. She was smart and funny and beautiful and I don't have to tell you how we were during our intimate times. She was all I wanted. Her husband was an abusive drunkard who couldn't sit still without a drink in his hand. He hit her children for the slightest infraction. She wanted out, but he had this invisible hold on her. She couldn't leave him. I convinced her that I would take her and the children away. We'd start over, safe, fresh. When I came to pick them up I found out that she'd been duping me the whole time. She'd been suckering me for money so she could supply her pig of a husband with money for booze when their cash ran out. They were screwing when I stopped by. I took out the girl first. She was the easiest because she was asleep and didn't make much noise. The boy came next. With the shower running the parents didn't hear a thing when I hit him in the head so hard that his skull caved in. It was as quick for him as I could make it. I snuck into the parents room quietly, saw them going at it. I shot them both in the head. Bam! It was so simultaneous that their bodies stayed locked together."

"I don't know what to say to that."

"I can see the shock on your face," the stranger said. "I was sentenced to death by electrocution, but when I died something amazing happened. I was free, finally free to live the way I wanted to. I heard about a funeral and possessed the dead man's body. I've been doing that ever since, keeping people away from this house and its occupants. I don't want to see anyone here but the four people I murdered. I want Beatrice and her worthless husband to know that their children breathed their last here. I want them to know that they'll never escape as long as I live. I'll never let them forget me or what they did to themselves and their children."

"Why carry all that hate around with you, though?"

"Why?" the man asked befuddled. "Maybe because it's what kept me going when everything else wanted to let go. It's my damn unfinished business!"

"Why did Jacob yell at me to get out then?" Sandra asked, almost to herself.

"What?"

"Jacob, the son. The other night I woke up freezing, Annie was in my bedroom but not asleep and I'm pretty sure Jacob yelled, "*Get out bitch!*"

"Sneaky little bastard," the man breathed. "Jacob has been a thorn in my side since I killed him. He knows that the house needs people to stay afloat. If no one purchases it and fixes it, it'll fall apart and won't be able to hold them here any longer. I can't buy the property, though. No matter who I turn into it doesn't seem as if any of them have the ability to purchase this piece of shit dwelling. I can only help renovate it when someone buys it."

"So if the home falls apart, their ghosts will be free to move on?"

"Exactly," the ghost replied with a Nick-like smile. "Since I don't plan on letting that happen, I was more than willing to let you have at it with your shitty remodeling."

"Well at least you give an honest opinion," Sandra said with a shiver. "Well then, I guess we should get the rest of this shit hole fixed, huh?"

"Yes," the man agreed. "I like the sound of that." He reached out a hand to run it down Sandra's arm. "I do like the look of you. All that pent up passion bubbling just under the surface. It's been a hell of a long time since a woman's interested me."

"I'll take that as a compliment, but I'll have to politely refuse."

"I figured you'd say that, with the girls in house and everything," the man chuckled. "Well now you know the story. Since you haven't run screaming for the hills yet I suppose it's a good assumption that I'll be back tomorrow to help you continue the repairs."

"Uh, sounds good," Sandra replied, still trembling.

"Alright," the man she could no longer think of as Nick, said. "Have a good night, Sandra."

Sandra waited for the man to get into Nick's truck and drive away before she set to work. "Annie!" Sandra called, listening to tiny feet on the floorboards.

"Yes mama?"

"Find Tiny and tell her to tell her family that we're going to set them free. Then get all your toys together, everything, and take it to the car."

"Why?"

"Just do it, trust mama, now," Sandra admonished her youngest daughter.

"Okay," Annie replied with an accepting shrug. Sandra told Jaime virtually the same thing, leaving out the bit about Tiny and all.

The girls did as they were asked. When Sandra knew they were huddled in the car she went through the house preparing the rooms, hallways, and stair case. She stood outside of it for a minute, wondering if what she was about to do was the right thing. With a big sigh, she struck a match and tossing it through the doorway,

124

watched as a massive blaze burned through the old wood and new construction with hungry, licking flames. She looked back at her girls, who watched from her station wagon. Life wouldn't be the same for them. Little Annie would miss her friend, but hopefully in time Sandra would be able to help her understand what had happened and why she'd burned their house down. Sandra finally turned and walked to the station wagon. Strapping her seat belt over her lap, she made sure the girls were buckled up. She put the keys in the ignition, but the car wouldn't start.

"Did you think I wouldn't know?" the stranger asked, his ghostly white face showing just outside Sandra's window.

"I hoped you wouldn't find out until tomorrow."

"You're a fool Sandra. You could have fixed this place up and lived here happily. Now I can see that things will have to get uncomfortable between us."

Sandra unbuckled her seat belt and got out, ordering her children to stay in the car. "Whatever you need to do you do to me, leave my girls alone."

"Oh, well, we'll see about that later, but for now, I need to put this fire out. You see, I can't let them leave. But I can't get a new body either, so you'll have to put the fire out yourself."

"I don't have anything to work with."

"Do I look as if I care? Put it out or you'll die a quick death," the man sneered.

"And what will killing me do? The house will still burn."

"Put it out!" the man yelled, furious.

"Screw you. You're a murdering bastard who preyed on a weak woman and her family. I'm not saying that her husband was saint, but she obviously didn't want to leave him. She was screwing him when you found them, after all."

"Beatrice wanted out!" the stranger continued to yell.

"I find it awfully telling, though, that the accounts I read all said that the woman and her lover died. They never mentioned the father of the children." The man looked up at her now, a look of pure, unadulterated hatred in his eyes.

"People make lots of mistakes you know."

"That they do, but not that many from different sources." Sandra pressed him as the house burned. "I think you're lying. I think you couldn't stand the thought that your wife was stepping out on you. I think you went into a rage when you came home and heard her with her lover. I think you killed them and then realized that your children would find out, so you killed them, too. I think you keep this old house here because you can't forgive yourself and assume that if you have to be tormented forever they should be too."

"You're wrong, you bitch."

"Nah, if I was wrong you'd be more convincing," Sandra sneered. "You see, I've known men like you. Controlling bastards who think their wives should submit to them about when they wipe their own ass. You want absolute control and when she doesn't give it, you use the back of your hand or your fist to teach her a lesson. You demand the use of her body for your gratification and show no remorse or love or affection. She found someone who cared for all of her, not just her flesh. You couldn't stand that, especially in your own home, so you killed them. You're a weak, no account asshole and the house burns."

"No!" the man said, but when he went to strike her, he found four angry ghosts staring him down.

"You lay a hand on her and we'll take your body with us into that house," Jacob threatened, his dark eyes angry.

"Yeah!" little Tiny said. "Annie's my friend. Sandra watched as the four ghosts dealt with one of their own. The house burnt to the ground, leaving on the foundation intact. Sandra drove her girls to the nearest hotel.

Epilogue

It took nearly a year to put a new house up. Sandra kept the original foundation in honor of the family that lost their lives in the home. She and the girls planted a tree and put a plaque in the ground commemorating the lives of Jacob, Beatrice, Trisha and Mason. The first night in the new house was a quiet one. Sandra knew she'd have to call the plumber in the morning so the faucets would quit dripping. If that was her only issue though, it wasn't so bad.

She passed Jaime's room, listening to the soft music that sifted out into the hallway. The house was set up virtually the same way the old house had been, but the room locations were different. Sandra moved on, picking up littered clothes and toys as she went. The girls, she knew, would be down soon enough to fight over who got which toys. Smiling, Sandra walked past Annie's room, taking a listen as she went.

"I know, but trust me, having a big sister isn't all it's cracked up to be either!" Annie lamented.

"Annie, who are you talking to?" Sandra asked, pushing the door open with her foot. Looking at her daughter, Sandra nearly fainted as the toys and clothes in her arms simply floated to the floor. Sitting across from her little girl was Tiny. Looking up, Sandra saw Jacob, Beatrice and Mason all standing in the room, each consumed with something until she spoke. When their dark eyes turned on her, Sandra knew that the haunting was just beginning.